THE SHADOW INSIDE

Jason J. Tavares

The Shadow Inside

Copyright © 2008 by Jason J. Tavares

ISBN-13: 978-1492114185
ISBN-10: 1492114189

Printed in the United States of America

www.facebook.com/authorjasonjtavares

jbnimbeljbquick@cox.net

WATCH

Jason J. Tavares

Movies

on

YouTube

Noise in the Kitchen

Eddie Thurber's Formidable Adversary

Eddie Thurber II Allies & Adversaries

DEDICATED

TO

Edmund V. Nolan, Sr.

and

Mildred L. Nolan

A dark figure or image cast on a surface by a body intercepting light, according to Random House *Webster's Dictionary*. In Swedish, it's called *skugga*, and in Spanish, it's called *sombra*, but in English, we say *shadow*. This phenomenon is not strange or mystical, and it isn't supernatural in any way. It's an everyday occurrence that most of us simply ignore. Over time, we become oblivious to things that we dismiss as trivial, especially when life is hectic, even for the average person. Now, what if those shadows that we choose to disregard each day decided to let us know they had a purpose? Wouldn't that change things a bit?

This story is about a boy named Nicholas Johansson, who took a shadow on a wall and made it a shadow inside. In 1978, after a massive wintry blast blanketed everything in the small state of Rhode Island, Nicholas Johansson made an incredible discovery during a tragic accident. Nicholas was very young but extremely large and strong for an eight-year-old child. He stood nearly five feet tall and weighed almost one hundred pounds. He had blonde hair and blue eyes, traits of his Swedish ancestry that traced back to the time of the Vikings.

The name Johansson had once struck fear in the hearts of all who spoke it or heard it. For many generations, the Johanssons were a family of powerful soldiers and great political leaders. Today, the Johanssons of Providence, Rhode Island, were a well-respected part of their community and a very happy family as a whole. Nicholas's parents always taught him to give back and be thankful for all the wonderful gifts that life had to offer. Nick's mom often told him that people forgot to be thankful more than they should, and that living an honest life and helping others will always be rewarding in the end. Karma remembers, she said. He did not fully understand all of his mom and dad's advice, but soon he would find out that what they preached was worth its weight in gold.

Nicholas was an intelligent boy. He enjoyed reading history, listening to rock 'n' roll, riding skateboards, and working out in the yard on cars with his dad. Nick's dad owned a body shop over in East Providence called The Torque Wrench. It was the cleanest shop in town, and its motto was "Consider It Fixed." People familiar with the auto business and the professionalism of The Torque Wrench thought it was a catchy motto, and it reassured new customers that his shop was the best choice for their auto needs.

People constantly mistook Nicholas's age, thinking he was several years older than he actually was, and they complimented his manners and the mature way he behaved toward everyone he made contact with. Even people who knew him would sometimes forget he was only eight years old. But despite his tough exterior, he did have a boyish side, though he only displayed it during story time with his mom. She could make up the most magnificent bedtime stories on any topic imaginable. Some nights she would tell a tale of dragons, and on another night she told of pirates or travels in outer space.

Looking back on his life, Nicholas would remember those days fondly. Those were the days of innocence, the days before sleepless nights and nervous days, before he was chosen to be a partner to a shadow who, in order to exist, made its home inside of his body and mind. He was an unsuspecting boy who would later be seized with an obsession like an illness that he had to find a cure for. "Nicholas would be forced to better understand his fear". His sense of sanity would occasionally escape him as his mind traveled to strange places in search of strength to conquer fear.

On one particular night, Nicholas's mother told him a tale about ghosts. She hadn't meant to scare Nicholas, but she delivered the tale with such vividness and enthusiasm that it left the boy a bit rattled. Afterward, he lay awake, looking for ghosts from the pages of his mother's story, but an hour later, he was fast asleep. It was a Thursday night, early in the month of December. Nicholas awoke shortly after two in the morning with a strong desire to raid the refrigerator for some of his mom's peanut butter and walnut cookies and a glass of milk. He wandered down the hall as quietly as he could, shuffling along in his size-eight-and-a-half fuzzy dog slippers.

Nicholas crept into the kitchen and carefully pried the fridge door open so the suction sound wouldn't wake his folks. He reached in and was able to grab three cookies and the jug of milk without making a single sound. He put one cookie in his mouth, one in the left pocket of his pajama bottoms, and the other in his shirt pocket. Crumbs would end up in his bed, but he only cared about satisfying his craving for a late-night snack.

He grabbed the biggest glass that he could from the cabinet next to the stove and slowly poured the milk until the glass almost overflowed like a bubbling volcano. Before he could recap the gallon jug, he froze like a statue. He could see the living room window from where he was standing in the kitchen by the refrigerator. Nicholas stared at the closed curtains. He saw the shadow of what seemed to be a large figure standing outside the window looking in.

The human-like silhouette cast by the moonlight was illuminated by the light of the open fridge door, so Nicholas carefully lowered the gallon of milk to the floor to prop the door open and maintain the light. The figure remained still, apparently unsuspecting, as Nicholas made his next move. Grabbing a steak knife from the knife rack on the kitchen shelf, he sank to the floor and crawled toward the side door. Nicholas eased the bolt open and turned the handle very slowly, exiting his house like a thief.

At this point he was out without his parents' permission, carrying a large knife and hunting a suspected burglar. And he was totally ruining his new slippers on the mud in the process. Suddenly the reality of the situation hit Nicholas. He felt the cold air of the winter's night on his face and the wetness seeping through his slippers. His heart pounded louder and louder. Despite the ice-cold temperature, he was sweating through his pajamas as if he were wearing a fur coat in South America in August.

He crouched lower and crept along the side of the house, sloshing through the mud and snow as he made his way to the far corner of the house. Once there, he hid behind a bush, only a few feet from the living room window where the predator lurked. Nicholas was initially apprehensive, but he took a deep breath and lunged around the corner, blade held high. To his surprise, nobody was there. The night air was quiet and crisp, and the muddy ground outside the window hadn't been disturbed in days.

Nicholas stood still, confused. His eyes were wide, and all he could hear was the thunderous beating of his heart. He accidentally dropped the knife as his body went limp from the shock. Why, he wondered, was nobody there? Nicholas let out a deep breath and then squatted down to search for the knife. As he stood up, he glanced at the window. The window looked normal, but on the opposite side of the glass, as if peering out from behind the curtain, was the very shadow that he'd seen when he was inside. But this time, whatever it was was inside looking out at him. Before Nicholas could scream, the light from inside his house faded to black. The figure was now indiscernible. It was as if it wanted to give Nicholas a glimpse, just enough to announce its arrival. Nicholas was beyond frantic. He ran screaming across the yard's uneven terrain, desperately trying to get back into the house to warn his parents of the possibly dangerous intruder.

Tears streamed down his cheeks. All he could think of as an explanation was that the ghost in his mother's bedtime story had somehow manifested itself in reality or was part of an awfully realistic dream. Upon making it to the door, Nicholas let out a final blood-curdling scream that his parents couldn't help but hear. In that same moment, he slipped on ice as he lunged up the stairs. The sharp steak knife was thrust deep into his left forearm. He ended up in a puddle of his own blood, lying lopsided on the icy concrete stairs. His adrenalin-filled body crashed down with such momentum that it had forced the cold blade in clean to the wooden handle. He also whacked his head in the process. Just as a brave warrior would do, Nicholas attempted to stand up, concerned only for his loved ones who were in danger. But his body did not respond to his brain's command.

The wound was severe. He lost blood so rapidly that he quickly lost consciousness. Luckily, Nicholas was blessed with a powerful set of lungs. Most of the neighbors heard his ghastly cry, as did his parents, who rushed to his aid only seconds after the incident. The neighbors from next door, Fred and Elaine Shyeetis, immediately came to Nicholas's aid as well. Mr. Shyeetis was so concerned that he had actually ran barefoot and shirtless straight from his warm bed out the door to answer the cry.

An ambulance came to rush Nicholas to the nearest emergency room. The emergency room staff was top of the line when it came to patient care. After lying unconscious for five hours and getting an amazing number of stitches, young Nicholas slowly began to open his eyes. His vision was blurry. The first person he saw, vaguely, was a very skinny, scruffy individual named Nurse Lanolin.

Nurse Lanolin was a forty-six-year-old Irishman and a barroom brawler who happened to enjoy his booze in his free time, along with busting heads, if the situation called for it. As a professional in the medical field, however, Nurse Lanolin spent his life caring for people. Perhaps he chose that profession out of guilt for putting so many people in the hospital when he was off duty.

Nurse Lanolin leaned over Nick's bed and asked in his scratchy voice, "How are you feeling?"

"I'm really tired. And I've got a headache and a sore left arm," Nicholas replied.

"Could you answer a trick question?" the nurse asked. Nicholas swallowed and then grinned, realizing that he now had a sore throat to add to his list of problems. Lanolin held up three fingers and a thumb. "How many fingers do you see?"

Nicholas described exactly what the nurse was displaying to him. "Three fingers and a thumb." Then he politely asked, "Could I please see my mom and dad? Are they okay?"

Nurse Lanolin smiled at Nicholas. "Your parents are perfectly fine. They're outside the door talking with the doctor. I'll go get 'em for ya."

Before stepping out of the hospital room, the nurse pointed back and winked at Nicholas, complimenting him for figuring out the trick so easily.

Mr. and Mrs. Johansson entered the room as soon as they were informed that their son was awake and communicating. The Johanssons were joined by their caring neighbors, Mr. and Mrs. Shyeetis and Mr. and Mrs. Meideros.

The Meideros family lived a few streets away, and their son Jimmy was a great friend of Nick's. Nick and Jimmy shared all the same interests, though only Nick's mother told stories at night before bed. Being guys, neither of them would admit that they liked being treated as little boys, so Nick never brought the topic of bedtime stories up in conversation. Jimmy was a few inches shorter and about thirty pounds lighter than Nicholas. He was your typical all-American boy growing up in what Nicholas referred to as "Sweat Pants Rhode Island." He added the title to the state's name in honor of all the fat people who shouldn't be wearing sweat pants and all the others who were too cheap to invest in belts.

Jimmy was the kind of guy who had a naturally friendly, honest smile and a winning personality to match. He was a very trustworthy guy who would stand by your side, no questions asked. Nicholas was proud of their friendship, and seeing Jimmy there when he needed him made the situation easier to tolerate. The room was now filled with the happy faces of family, friends, and medical staff.

Nick's dad sat on the edge of the bed. "Are you okay?" he asked.

Nicholas sat in silence because he truly did not know how to answer that question. His mind was a bit cloudy. He was beginning to realize how he ended up in the hospital and what he had seen in the window. A moment later he looked over at his mother, as if oblivious to his father's question. "Did you see him?" he asked her.

His mother's eyes grew wide and glassy. "Did I see who?"

"Did you see the man in the living room? The man that was watching me? The man I chased after? The man that closed our refrigerator door while I watched the light go black from outside the window?" Nicholas's voice rattled as he grew more upset. His breathing was heavy, and his face was pale from the mental and physical exhaustion of his ordeal. Everyone was silent as they patiently listened to what Nicholas had to say. The poor boy had gone to bed the night before slightly rattled from a bedtime story. Now he was a paranoid mess unaware of what he would see next.

Moments after Nicholas repeatedly questioned his parents, Nurse Lanolin cleared the room of everyone except family members. Room B37 became a place of concern, a place where the tension alone could produce enough energy to jumpstart an eighteen-wheeler. Nick's mother sat on one side of the bed holding her son's hand, and his father sat on the other.

They were both in shock over their son's condition. Mrs. Johansson spoke softly and calmly to Nicholas in an attempt to elicit more information and possibly unravel the story of what happened to him.

Mr. Johansson said, "Just relax, son, and explain what you saw."

Nick's mom had a tear running down her face as she petted her son's hand, desperate for a clue. "Were you sleepwalking during a nightmare?" she asked. "Is that why you grabbed a knife and then slipped on the icy stairs? Is that a possibility?"

His father's face showed his hopelessness, as if he was in personal agony or felt deep down that he should be the person in the hospital bed instead of his only son. Nicholas just lay in the bed, silent. He too had a tear running down his cheek. Nicholas had never seen his parents so upset, and he'd never felt so helpless in his entire life.

The room around him began to read like a page from a novel. Musty hospital smells reached his nose, and the cheap fabric of the sheets felt uncomfortable. The walls of his room were painted yellow and green. The only things that set off the dreariness were all the fancy lights, wires, and machines attached to him. Glancing at the contraptions led his eye to the blanket draped over him. It was kind of brown, with yellow zigzags placed here and there.

Nicholas's father then let out a deep sigh of irritation, the irritation of still not having any notion of how these events came to be. He glanced at his wife, and she noticed the aggravation inscribed in his face. She lowered her eyes as he stood up abruptly, bumping the bed as he rose. Mr. Johansson stared down at Nicholas. Pointing at him, he snapped a stiff order in a stern voice: "Young man, explain the entire story right this minute!" He received no response. He repeated the command, but before he could say another word, Mrs. Johansson demanded that he stop his questioning.

"Our son has survived a violent, life-threatening accident. When he's ready to confide in us, he will. But in the meantime, leave him alone."

My mom is no joke, Nicholas thought as he watched her defend his right to silence. Nick's dad did not answer her. He stood there, dazed for a second, then he glanced at Nicholas and gave him a slight head nod and a tiny half grin. He stuffed his hands in his pants pockets and shuffled his feet along the yellow linoleum as he slowly walked out the door and down the corridor. Nicholas was made uneasy by his mom's next action. She kissed him on the cheek and tried to reassure him. "Your dad loves you so much that he's having trouble dealing with the pain of you being hurt. But no matter what took place, all that matters is that you're healthy and safe. That's all that matters to us." This filled Nick's heart with a joyful understanding of how dedicated and devoted his parents truly were and how much they loved him.

Nick's dad reentered the room and apologized for his sternness. He also informed his wife and son that while he was in the hallway, the doctor informed him that Nicholas could be released as early as tomorrow afternoon. The only stipulation is that he remain under close supervision at home for the first couple of days in order to monitor his healing process. Nurse Lanolin then came in the room. "Don't worry," he said reassuringly, "your son will be in good hands until he is released to go home." He also added, "Your friends who visited earlier left their blessings and said they will be in touch soon." Nurse Lanolin then gave Nicholas a dose of pain medication to help him sleep comfortably. The nurse smiled at Nick and said, "You'll have happy dreams and wake up well rested."

The Johanssons said their temporary good-byes to their son, who was already feeling the soothing effects of the pain medication. His mother told him, "You need to rest, as the nurse requested. And tomorrow night before bedtime, you'll get two stories instead of one." He thought to himself, I hope the stories aren't about ghosts. Within moments, Nicholas felt one eyelid droop a little. The other followed shortly after. The medication made sleep inevitable, but

he fought the sleep monster long enough to see his parents walk out the door together holding hands.

As soon as the door closed behind them, Nurse Lanolin followed.

Nicholas then forced open his eyes and took one more glance around the perimeter of the room that was to be his home for the next day or two. There were no people to be seen in the room. But then he saw the shadow of a girl on the wall as she seemed to pass by the door on the inside of the room. Nicholas was now more frightened than a cornered kitten. The shadow paused and stood there. She was watching him, he thought, and she noticed his panicked reaction.

He felt very weak and alone, as if everyone had abandoned him. Nick knew deep inside that this was not true. But he had suffered so much physical and mental trauma that his mind was clouded and he seemed unable to think rational, clear thoughts. If he let out a scream, help would arrive, but would they think he was insane? Would the medical staff believe him if he told them he was seeing a shadow of a girl in an empty room, a shadow without a body to project it? At this point, any absurdity that Nicholas might sputter would be attributed to the medication, the trauma, and the fact that he was only eight years old. Nicholas had become a victim of circumstance, entangled in strange, inexplicable phenomena. His body was on the verge of submission. Dreamland was the next stop on his ride.

The man in the corner was ringing the bell to indicate the end of round fifteen in this heavyweight bout. Nicholas Johansson, the exhausted ex-champion, tried to peel himself off the canvas after a vicious knockdown. Despite the medication and all his bumps and bruises, Nicholas's brain wasn't ready to quit. He squeezed, wrenched, and twitched until his eyelashes at last parted a fragment of an inch. That was all Nicholas hoped for. The battle was a victory. Taking one last look around the room, he didn't see one single shadow in the room—he saw two.

Then the curtains came down for the night, tightly closed over a set of tired young eyeballs that had seen enough to last a lifetime. Family members and friends were en route to their homes, while the medical staff made their usual morning rounds through the facility. Nicholas Johansson's room grew very, very quiet. All that could be heard was the peaceful, steady breathing of the resting young man. The lights had been turned off to give him an atmosphere more conducive to sleep. Despite the privacy of his single room, all eyes were on Nicholas Johansson.

Shadow Chapter
NUMBER
Two...

The sun came up the following morning, and the temperature was unpredictably a freaky fifty-two degrees. Rhode Island winters seldom hit the forties, never mind the fifties. Outside of Nick's hospital room window, icicles were beginning to melt. Birds were chirping a melody as if they were welcoming in the ray of sunshine that was beaming on the wall. A few hours had passed since the sun rose, and Nicholas had just opened his eyes and looked about the hospital room that he'd forgotten he was in. He scraped the crust out of his eyes and let out a long yawn. He began to stretch, but was quickly reminded of the pain in his left arm. His headache from the head whack wasn't as bad today, but he was still fatigued from the medication. Nurse Lanolin had done a great job bandaging up his arm. He ran his good hand over the stiff protective dressing that covered the wound. He then wondered to himself how cool the scar would look once it was completely healed. That made him think of all the stories that he could tell the other kids around town about what took place when he went hunting the stalker.

The sounds of the hospital were much clearer today, now that the ringing in his ears had subsided. Nicholas could hear talking in the hall, footsteps, and the sound of scratchy food carts and hospital beds being shuffled around. He didn't even pretend to understand half of the medical mumbo-jumbo that was being blabbed outside of his room. Nicholas was perfectly content to twiddle his thumbs and daydream while he stared at the ceiling, waiting for his folks to arrive to take him home. Lying in the lumpy bed, he began to feel comfortable in the hospital room. As he recapped the chain of events that led to his hospitalization, he convinced himself that his mom may be right. Maybe he had, in fact, been sleepwalking. Perhaps the shadow outside of his living room window was a figment of his imagination, along with the shadows in the hospital room. Or they could all have been particles of a dream that he hadn't fully wakened from when he went in pursuit of cookies and milk. Either way, he felt that he could dismiss the situation as a simple brain glitch where the wires may have accidentally crossed.

Nicholas then looked down at his right wrist and examined the medical tag attached to it. He was looking for potential flaws in the spelling of his name or date of birth. From what he could see, it was fine. Nurse Lanolin interrupted his research when he entered the room accompanied by an odd-looking man whom Nicholas hadn't seen before during his brief stay at the hospital. The man was completely bald and approximately six feet tall. He didn't make many facial expressions other than an occasional roll of the eyes whenever Nurse

Lanolin said anything slightly out of the ordinary. His complexion was exceptionally pale, blending in with his white lab coat as if it was a continuation of his skin. Creepy was the only word Nicholas could think of to describe this man. He was like an alien disguised as a human being in a sci-fi movie. What bothered Nicholas the most were the doctor's eyes. At least he had two of them instead of one planted in the middle of his head like a Cyclops. But even though their placement was correct, they were still bone chilling and very hard to stare at. This guy's large eyes were as blue as the ocean in the Bahamas. And their contrast with the paleness of his skin made them seem piercing and calculating, as if they could slice through the bullshit of the greatest con artist. He probably had the power to see if you were naughty or nice, kind of like Santa Claus but without the reindeer pulling a sleigh. Nicholas could feel himself transfixed by the man's stare during the ten or so seconds since he'd entered the room. Breaking the stare was his only choice. He decided to focus on the gentleman's name tag instead. The tag said "Dr. Chenker." The doctor stepped up to Nicholas as he lay in the bed. Nicholas expected the worst, not knowing what the man was about to say.

"My name is Dr. Chenker, but you can call me DC for short, if you like. How are you feeling today, Nicholas?" And suddenly a completely relaxing feeling crashed over Nicholas like a huge wave spraying mist into the air. "Is it okay if I look at your arm?" Nick then learned that at a hospital, if you pause too long before you answer a question, the answer must automatically be yes. Dr. Chenker examined, mumbling something to Nurse Lanolin, who took notes on a clipboard. The doctor proceeded to ask Nicholas to follow the red beam of his penlight with just his eyes.

He was then asked to recite the alphabet and count to twenty-five slowly. These questions seemed silly to an eight-year-old boy, but then, Nicholas thought, who am I to question a doctor. For all Nicholas knew, Dr. Chenker could have been an escaped lunatic from a house for the criminally insane just posing as a medical professional. One lesson that Nicholas was completely sure of was that he would never leave the house again unless he checked with Mom and Dad first.

The evaluation continued with a series of questions pertaining to how Nicholas felt physically and how he felt in his home life. Nick answered the questions to the best of his ability, attempting to be polite. As the questioning proceeded, however, he began to understand that they were less about his arm or head injury and more about his view of his parents. Nick was only an eight-year-old boy, but his understanding of human behavior and logic was that of a teenager. This strange man was cross-examining him without his parents' consent! Before the doctor asked his next question, Nicholas cut in and asked, "How long have you been a shrink?" Dr. Chenker looked furious as he again locked the boy's eyes in a stare. They both exchanged frosty looks. Finally, the doctor asked Nicholas if he was uncomfortable for some reason. The man's voice sounded so peaceful and concerned, it made Nicholas want to vomit. Nick felt the urge to fight brewing inside himself, just as he had when he saw the first shadow outside his living room window. This young man was intelligent, quick witted, and cunning. He was in the midst of a medical deception and he knew it. Identifying the truth behind unclear accidents resulting in serious wounds was this man's specialty. In Nick's eyes, he didn't deserve to be called doctor, so Nicholas asked Nurse Lanolin if he would ask the liar to please leave. Nurse Lanolin looked more shocked than the doctor.

When a police officer pulls you over in traffic, thought Nicholas, he at least has the professional courtesy to identify himself before he questions you. In a situation like that, you know the nature of the interaction from the outset. Sure, maybe on occasion a policeman will pop out from behind a building to detain a criminal. But even during an elaborate process like that, the arresting official never pretends he's something he's not, unless he's undercover. While these comparisons were bouncing around Nicholas's mind, Nurse Lanolin didn't relay the condescending statement to the doctor for Nicholas, but the doctor had already accepted the fact that his cover was blown and was ready to exit the room. The boy didn't let him slip his tail that easily. "May I ask you one last question, Dr. Chenker?"

Without turning around, the doctor replied, "By all means, Nicholas."

Nicholas paused for a moment in order to create noticeable discomfort for the two men. Tension was so heavy, a knife couldn't cut it.

Nick then calmly asked, "How long have you been a psychiatrist, Dr. Chenker?"

Nurse Lanolin's mouth parted slightly as he took a step back, giving the doctor the floor to battle wits with the eight-year-old boy. Though he turned around nonchalantly with a hand in his pocket, his nostrils flared as he replied, "Twelve years." His expression was that of an overconfident chess player who'd been beaten for the first time at his own game by an unlikely adversary. Nicholas said nothing at all in response. He just smirked. The doctor offered no departing sentiments. He simply obtained his clipboard from the nurse and left the room. Nicholas did not brag about his small, satisfying victory, but the twisted grin on his face basically told the tale. Nurse Lanolin waited until the doctor was gone, then he told Nicholas that on behalf of the entire staff he wanted to say thank you.

Nicholas then asked the nurse, "Would you care to answer a question that's on the mind of a poor, sick little boy?"

"I can't imagine what it is, so just lay it on me, man."

"When's breakfast?" Nicholas asked. "I'm totally starved. When am I going home? And when is the real doctor going to examine me?"

"You're one funny son of a bitch," the nurse replied. "Food is on its way. You'll get the answers to all your questions as soon as the real doctor arrives."

Nicholas thanked the man as they both shared a laugh together, then the nurse headed out to fill Nick's requests.

Nicholas had experienced almost every emotion imaginable over the last twenty-four hours. He'd been on an emotional train ride with stops at pain, fear, anger, sadness, fatigue, confusion, curiosity, hunger, and, last but not least, deception and deceit. What he wanted more than anything was to be back home with a full stomach after one of his mom's great dinners. After dinner, Nicholas often liked to lie in bed, throwing his basketball in the air, bouncing it off of the ceiling, and staring at the map of the world that was glued to his bedroom wall. He knew that he wanted a life of travel and adventure after he was done with school. His dad bought him a subscription to *National Geographic* a few years ago. After reading about ancient fossils, historical findings, and architecture, his life's true ambition was cast in stone. He knew what he was wired for, and he was totally prepared to pursue that dream.

Nicholas looked out the window where he had seen and heard the birds chirping earlier. The beam of light that was cast on the wall earlier was now so solid it was almost glowing in radiance, its beam penetrating the dirty Plexiglas window. Thousands of particles of dust swarmed through the transparent cone of light. To most people, dust is a nuisance that should be disposed of before people start sneezing, but to Nicholas it looked like another world. The dust resembled tiny stars and moons, each illuminated by the light of the window. Maybe they were unknown galaxies that hadn't been discovered yet, or particles of a lost world that exploded eons ago. Either way, imagining what hasn't been discovered was very interesting to Nicholas.

Each of the swarming dust particles swirled around as if it had a purpose or an ulterior motive like Dr. Chenker. Was their motive to keep Nicholas's attention long enough for him to see something, something unbelievable, something meant for his select eyes only? Suddenly, a shadowy silhouette of a woman stepped out from nothingness, materializing like a phantom on the wall. From what Nicholas could see, she was definitely naked. Her outline and three-dimensional curves spoke for themselves. She was approximately five feet tall, give or take a couple of inches. She glided briskly about, once she assumed that she had Nicholas's full attention. The elegant dance she was performing allowed her long straight hair to flip around as she twirled. It appeared to be almost as long as her spine, ending near the curve of her lower back. Nicholas remembered that she had been on the wall during his first evening at the hospital.

I was obviously delusional then, and I'm obviously delusional now, Nicholas thought. He kicked himself for scaring off the shrink. He told himself that shadow people are not real. He repeated this several times, moving his lips as he repeated the statement out loud. He gripped the hospital sheets tightly with his good hand while he watched her gradually dance toward him. He was shaking so profusely that he lost control and peed in his bed out of sheer fright. The shadow was only a few feet away from him now. All of a sudden, his body jerked in fear. His teeth cut through his bottom lip, and blood began trickling down his chin.

Young Nicholas was not alone, however. Dr. Chenker was spying on Nicholas from the hallway, peering through the hospital room door. His cold eyes bulged out of his pale head as he saw the boy transfixed in horror, staring at a sight that wasn't there. From where the doctor was standing, he wouldn't have been able to see the shadow anyway. Not everyone can see them, including Nick's parents. They were standing next to the doctor in the hall, viewing their son's sad spectacle. It looked as if he was losing his mind. Dr. Chenker informed Nick's parents of their slight argument earlier and suggested they arrange for psychiatric treatment.

Nicholas was unaware that during the night he'd had nightmares and had thrashed about, screaming in his sleep. His eyes would open wide, and he would sit up in bed as if he was awake. Then suddenly his body would collapse back onto the bed in complete silence, as if he'd never moved a muscle. Dr. Chenker was well aware of the erratic behavior Nicholas was displaying. He gave Nick's parents a complicated medical term for the condition, but they didn't understand until he broke it down and explained to them that it was schizophrenia. He then told them that he's an expert in this field, although he'd not documented any cases among children.

"Extreme shock," Dr. Chenker said to Mr. and Mrs. Johansson, "can ignite a variety of odd patterns of behavior in people of all ages. The body reacts without argument to any and all orders that the brain sends it. If a certain impulse or stimulation is remembered from a traumatic event in a person's life, that same stimulus may later trigger actions related to the cause. In Nicholas's case, he was apparently very scared during or before his accident. Now, as a result, he may experience odd behavior while he's awake or asleep. This will last for as long as the body needs it to last in order to deal with the mental pain. Hopefully, in time, the body and brain can successfully filter out the cause and bring it to a psychological place where it can be dealt with in a less disturbing way."

The doctor then handed the Johanssons a business card that read "Dr. Reid Anderson, Child Psychiatrist." Nicks parents glanced at the card, then asked Dr. Chenker if he thought Nicholas could be treated successfully. Smiling a friendly smile and hiding a smidgen of embarrassment, the doctor said, "I have a confession to make before I answer that question. Your son was able to identify me as a psychiatrist within the first few minutes of our conversation." Nicholas had not seen this human, friendly side of Dr. Chenker when they first met. If he had, his first impression probably would have been better, and the doctor, feeling more secure about his methods, would not be referring the Johanssons to another psychiatrist. "Nicholas," the doctor continued, "is very clever for an eight-year-old boy. He's on an intellectual level higher than ninety percent of children his age. The first impression I made on Nicholas was not a positive one. This negative first impression would only cloud his recovery process, creating an atmosphere filled with emotional barriers toward his psychiatrist. Dr. Reid Anderson comes highly recommended. I could furnish you with a distinguished list of people in all walks of medicine who would totally agree with my assessment. Since Nicholas has never met Dr. Anderson, their first meeting could take place outside of a hospital room, giving Nick a chance to meet his doctor in a more comfortable setting." Dr. Chenker then apologized to the Johanssons for not being upfront with their son when they were introduced. He told them that he only told Nicholas that he was a doctor, without specifying whether he was a pediatrician or psychiatrist.

The doctor expressed his gratitude for their patience, wishing the best to their son and a speedy recovery. He then excused himself and said he would send the pediatrician, Dr. Fernando Rivard, to speak with them about Nicholas's arm and head wounds. Before walking away, he reiterated the fact that Reid Anderson is a gifted man in his field. Meeting him in person and being in his presence is the only way to totally elaborate on the fact that he's simply the best. In the meantime the Johanssons couldn't help but wonder how their quiet, respectful son had managed to rattle a grown man so easily.

The pediatrician soon arrived at room B37 and got down to the nuts and bolts, instructing the Johanssons how to care properly for Nicholas once he went home. After their discussion, Dr. Rivard suggested that Mr. and Mrs. Johansson have a seat in the waiting room until Nicholas was dressed and ready to leave. Despite his advice, the two of them hung around the hallway outside of Nicholas's room in case he needed assistance. When the curious parents looked through the glass in their son's hospital room door, they were surprised. Nicholas, who was already fully dressed, was again engaged in more odd behavior. He'd taken a crutch from the closet and was poking and tapping on the wall at the far corner of the room near the window. From what his parents could see, it looked like he was looking for a secret passageway or a hollow spot where something could be hidden. Nicholas, on the other hand, thought he knew exactly what he was doing: he was investigating the area where he'd seen the shadow girl. Mr. and Mrs. Johansson simply could not understand their son's peculiar behavior. Nicholas took three quick steps back while they watched. His back was to them the entire time. Holding the crutch in his good arm, Nicholas raised it over his head as if he was ready to defend himself or hit something. Then he slowly lowered the crutch until it was resting loosely by his side. It then fell out of Nicholas's hand, hitting the floor beneath him. Nick stepped forward and reached out toward the wall, waving at it with his good hand. It looked as if he was trying to cast shadows on the wall.

Nick's parents watched silently. Their son's insanely strange behavior went on for almost five minutes. Then Nicholas seemed startled by something that he saw. When he jumped backwards, he accidentally stepped on the crutch, lost his balance, and fell to the floor flat on his butt. Luckily, he didn't produce any new injuries or complicate the situation by damaging old ones. The Johanssons rushed into the room to rescue their son and to see if he was all right. Nick's dad helped him up to a standing position and made sure he was okay. He was a little dusty from the floor and a bit shaken, but he was otherwise fine. His mother and father squatted in front of him, pleading and begging for answers from their son. All they wanted was some understanding of the situation.

Nicholas had to lower his eyes to look down at his parents. Rising up from behind them on the empty wall was the shadow of the girl. The boy inhaled so deeply that he began gasping for air as he lurched backwards, pointing at the wall behind his parents. His parents immediately spun around to see what had startled their son, but there was nothing there. Nicholas took another step back, this time with his hand over his mouth and his eyes closed. His body was shaking so much that his mom could just barely hold him still.

Mr. Johansson yelled, "Nicholas, what is it? What's frightening you? We can't see it!" His mother, horrified, began to cry. Tears streamed down her concerned face. She was holding her son tightly, trying to calm him down. All she wanted was to protect him from the danger that she could not see. Nicholas reopened one eye while still deep in his mother's hug. He watched the female shadow reach out from the wall. She was now on the other side of the room near the bed he'd slept in. She latched onto the bedrail with both hands. Two other shadow figures appeared on the wall. They grabbed her and dragged her off of the bedrail and into thin air. She never made a sound, but when her ghostly hands released the bedrail, it made a snapping sound that rattled throughout the room. The jaws of Nicholas's parents almost literally hit the floor when they heard the sound reflected off the bare walls. Nicholas stood there with his hand still over his mouth. He was motionless and expressionless, unable to offer any explanation to his parents. Judging by the grim looks on their faces, they were also very scared. Logic and reason could not explain this. And only love and patience toward each other could pull them through. The family huddled together, holding each other close. They watched as the vibrations of the hollow metal bedrail eventually came to a halt. Nick's parents did not see any shadows on the wall, but what they'd heard had scared them just the same. They quickly gathered all of Nicholas's things and left the hospital room as fast as humanly possible.

The Johansson family attempted to go on living a normal life, as if nothing had happened. The Johanssons have always been strong, optimistic people instilled with the notion that despite the circumstance nothing is too massive to confront or defeat. Optimism and strength are fantastic qualities to possess, but sometimes even the strongest souls can become pessimistic when confronted by the supernatural or unexplainable. In this case, only time would tell.

Shadow Chapter
NUMBER
Three...

With the support of his family, Nicholas held himself together. It was a difficult time in their lives. His parents might have been less capable of coping with their son's new behavior had it not been for the extreme kindness of their new family friend, Dr. Reid Anderson. The young, brilliant child psychiatrist had been referred to them by Dr. Chenker while Nick was recovering in the hospital.

During their first visit with him, he introduced himself as Dr. Reid Anderson, but as Nicholas's visits came and went, he dissolved the formality and asked Nicholas to call him by his first name. There was nothing unusual in this. Medical personnel, athletics coaches, and college professors often use this simple tactic, establishing professional boundaries to build respect and then allowing the relationship to eventually turn into a friendship. First impressions, after all, are normally a key factor when people decide whether they like someone.

Reid met with Nicholas the morning after he was discharged from the hospital. Their first appointment was brief. It was more or less an introduction to establish guidelines for what the doctor expected to accomplish during their sessions together. Nicholas instantly liked Reid and considered him a man of unrestricted honesty. His problem-solving techniques never revolved around popping mind-altering pills from a bottle as a quick-fix cure.

Each session built on the previous one, adding new topics as the conversation progressed. Reid never questioned Nicholas's actions at the hospital or the accident that landed him there in the first place. The man simply enjoyed listening to what children had to say. In fact, he felt that children see the world from a perspective that we sometimes forget as adults.

Dr. Anderson was only twenty-four, but he carried himself as if he was a mature forty. Some of his physical characteristics attributed to this illusion. He was very thin and not very tall. His salt-and-pepper hair was cut slightly above his ears on the lower portion of his hairline. Sporadic sprinkled pieces of white specs were scattered throughout his head like tiny snowflakes. The remainder of his hair was worn short in a military style. Nicholas noticed that Reid occasionally wore glasses but never wore a tie at all. The good doctor also had perfect, pearly white teeth. His teeth were so perfect, they almost appeared animated when he smiled. And with Nicholas around, the doctor smiled a lot. The boy would often catch him off guard with his witty, well-thought-out comments and questions. With their strong bond and Reid's likable, animated qualities, it's no wonder a boy of eight would find him great.

Nicholas visited Dr. Anderson twice a week for one-hour sessions, a pattern that would continue for many years to come. The doctor taught Nicholas, talking in spurts but always in a cohesive manner. The lessons were of his own design, formulated for each patient as the doctor got to know him or her. Facing fears and overcoming obstacles were usually the main objectives in his very successful theories of psychiatry. At the end of the session, Dr. Anderson would leave the patient with small tasks or goals to complete in order to involve the individual in curing themselves. Dr. Reid's motto was: "If answers are what someone desires, the best person to answer the questions is the individual asking them." Its proven success spoke for itself.

Although Reid did not exactly know what Nicholas was dealing with, he had a hunch it bordered on the supernatural. He tailored the boy's tasks according to that hypothesis. Each week that passed seemed a step in a positive direction. Dr. Anderson tested his methods on many levels. One exercise involved altering Nicholas's sleeping patterns. He had Nicholas sleep, for example, in his living room instead of his bedroom, but only when he felt most comfortable. This allowed the boy to challenge his mind by going against the grain when he felt safe. Another exercise was to create focal points whenever he was confused or frightened. Focal points are simply a fixed area to look at when you need to gather your thoughts and assess a situation of any magnitude. Focal points exist all around us, ranging from a picture on the wall to a telephone pole on the side of the road. Knowing where to find one and how to use them makes it easier to work through disturbing situations.

One afternoon, Nicholas was sweeping out the garage for his father. He was preparing to open the garage door to allow in the light and see if he missed any spots. In the midst of his action, however, his attention was diverted by a shadow on the wall that seemed to be watching his every move. Nick calmly rested the broom against his father's workbench. Swallowing the lump that was jammed in his throat, he looked out the window and focused on the tree in the yard and the squirrels that were playing in it. The tree was on the east side of the garage, and he'd last seen the shadow on the west. This focal point allowed Nicholas to literally turn his back on his fear so that he could direct his attention elsewhere. This was truly a test of Reid Anderson's instruction. After a few seconds of relaxed breathing and continuous focus on the point he'd selected, Nicholas gathered his thoughts and turned around. He then put both hands on the workbench and let out a deep sigh of relief. Sensing the room was empty, he strolled around the garage. Ignoring his fear, he placed himself directly in the spot where he saw the figure, but still he sensed nothing. His focus was broken when a mouse scurried across the floor in front of him, almost touching the tip of his work boot. Nick watched the small creature run into a tiny crawl space that led to the outside. Suddenly, the entire pegboard of tools came crashing off of the wall behind him and slammed onto the concrete. The floor was covered with hammers and saws, rakes and shovels. A small pegboard shelf also broke off, scattering nails and screws in all directions. All of Nicholas's hard work was gone in a blink of an eye. He had just swept the garage, and he and his dad had only recently installed the pegboard. Nick was so startled that he jumped clear off the floor, turned and faced the mess. The board had been constructed to hold at least one hundred pounds, so unless the tools jumped off the wall, they had to have been torn off. The pile of rubble was not a pretty site. Suddenly the garage door began to rise on its own. Nick crept toward it in sheer amazement. The wind outside was picking up, blowing dirt and leaves into the already messy garage.

Dr. Anderson refrained from informing Nick's parents that he suspected something paranormal was involved in their son's life. Reid understood, of course, that Nicholas was a minor, but in this rare case he held strictly to the rule of doctor-patient confidentiality. Nor was the doctor going to cross the lines between science and monsters under the bed. His practice was his life, but the life of this boy was worth the risk of losing that. He didn't want to make the wrong diagnosis, but how do you tell concerned parents that their only son can see strange things that may be real?

*****

Over five years had passed since Reid and Nicholas started working together. Nick had matured into a confident and very large teenage boy. At the age of thirteen, he was five foot ten and weighed nearly one hundred and eighty pounds. Dr. Anderson was ready to advance more quickly. Nicholas, he thought, had crawled and walked and was now ready to run. But Nicholas did not leak his true inner thoughts to Reid. Inside he was quite lonely, to say the least. He was still homeschooled and still seeing shadows here and there, more often than he'd care to admit. Nick knew that the doctor was paid to listen to his problems. But they were such good friends that he just didn't want to burden the guy with what was really going on in his life.

When Nick wasn't hanging out at the doctor's office, he spent his time with Jim Meideros. Jim, who stood by his side in the hospital when he was hurt at the age of eight, was now attending junior high school in the city. A few times a week, he would stop by Nick's house to play Atari or go into the woods and discuss chicks. Occasionally they'd light up a few cigarettes and try to impress each other by taking long, deep drags and not exhaling.

Jim was catching up to Nick in height, but he was still three or four inches shorter. He always wore a Led Zeppelin jean jacket with the fallen angel sewn on the back. The sleeveless jacket was very faded and ripped in places. Underneath it he wore a black leather jacket like a biker would wear. His jeans were also worn, but that was stylish in the eighties. Black combat boots were his shoe of choice, with jeans tucked in tight. Nicholas's parents never thought to question whether Jim was turning into a punker because of his excessive wardrobe. His demeanor was always very respectful, and he had a kind smile that basically let adults know that it was just a teenage phase.

Nick's style wasn't much different from Jim's at this point in his stressful young life. He always wore sunglasses so he could ignore the shadows that he didn't want to discuss. Black was his color from head to toe, including his steel-toed work boots. Plain black T-shirts, black jeans, and a long black coat. Nick's bangs hung past his chin, almost completely covering his eyes. Dr. Anderson and Jim Meideros were his only real friends outside of his folks.

There were days when Nicholas wanted to tell all of them that he was victimized by shadows or ghosts. He knew the doctor thought he was making progress, but all the doctor was doing was furnishing him with ammo to fight the battle. What Nicholas wanted was a cure for what had plagued and tortured him the past five years. Often he wondered if the doctor understood his true problem, even though he hadn't said a word about it. That may have been true, but Nicholas never questioned Reid, and Reid never questioned Nicholas about what was really on his mind.

One Tuesday afternoon in March 1984, Nick and Jim decided to attend a movie at a local low-budget theater. After that, they grabbed a burger and began their walk home. While they walked, they discussed the new equipment that they needed for sewer sloshing. "Sewer sloshing" is a term Nicholas invented to describe what Jimmy used to call "sewer diving." Nick decided this one day when he realized that they never really dove; they actually just sloshed around in the sewage under the streets of Providence. From that day forward, the new name stuck.

When they went sewer sloshing, the boys wore waist-high boots, raincoats, and long gloves that they stole from a toxic waste plant that Jim's uncle worked at. Other items necessary for proper sloshing were a miner's hat that had an operational light and a long stick for balance. You never knew what or who you would run into in the sewer. There were spots in the sewer where the stick served more for killing rats than balance. Both guys always loaded up on water, cigarettes, and beef jerky in case they became lost, hungry, or both during their sloshing. Inspecting each other's gear was also a priority before they ventured into the underground pit of filth and stench.

Who's to say why boys of all ages enjoy nasty, germ-filled adventures? They just do. It's not a topic that needs to be analyzed or questioned. They stash their sewer sloshing gear in the ruins of an old fireplace a few streets over from Jim's house. This way, the kids are happy, and the parents don't have to worry.

After they were done in the sewer, they usually cleaned their gear with a hose at a car wash. On this particular day, they were both very excited. Jim was able to find two large military-issue rucksacks with frames at a yard sale for only twenty bucks. These were perfect for carrying their gear. And to top things off, they were heading off to enter the sewer at a new insertion point near the railroad tracks, where there was a bunch of sewer caps with ladders underneath.

To a teenager, even solid metal sewer caps are claimable items, and steel underground ladders cemented to walls are fair game for anyone. The definition of personal property changes meaning pretty quickly once most people turn eighteen years of age, or at least it should. Removing the three-inch-thick lid from the ground wasn't as easy as they thought. Once it was out of the way, however, they suited up, inspected each other's gear, and entered. Jim gave the above world one more scan to see if they were being watched by police, parents, or other kids. The last thing they needed was to get busted for trespassing. Once down the ladder, they turned on their helmet lights and proceeded to slosh through two feet of muck. Each tunnel led to another in a maze of endless corridors filled with rusty pipes and odd noises.

During this little getaway, Jim was hoping he could discuss this chick that he was thinking of asking to the school dance. The beautiful young lady's name was Katrina. From the moment Jim laid eyes on her in homeroom, he knew she was the only girl for him. Jim knew he couldn't tell Nick all the mushy crap that he was really feeling, so instead he told Nick that she'd asked him to the dance. Toughening up the story is a good way for an insecure heterosexual male to express feelings about a special woman to another man. Every guy has been there at some point in his life, and at some point in his life the woman has seen right through it. Nicholas listened and sloshed, listened and sloshed, while Jim did a bad job of not spilling his guts.

"Have you even spoken to her yet?" Nick asked.

"Haven't you been listening to a word I said?"

Nicholas stopped walking and looked Jim in the eye. "I heard every word. The moral of the story is that you need to lift your skirt, grab your balls, and take her to the dance." Nick then proceeded ahead.

Jim just laughed, accepting his best friend's odd form of encouragement as the okay to ask her out. A couple hundred feet later, Jim asked Nick, "When are you going to get yourself a girl?"

Nicholas was quiet for a moment. "I've been talking to a local girl since I was eight years old." Nicholas made no eye contact as he said this.

Jim was curious why Nicholas had never mentioned this mysterious girl before. "How come you never told me?" he asked in an arrogant, disbelieving tone. "What's her name?"

"The girl's name is Lynn," Nick replied.

Jim laughed and said, "Lynn who?"

Nicholas got up in Jim's face and said, "I don't give a shit what you believe or don't believe. Her name is Lynn. We like each other … end of story."

Jim had never seen Nicholas get angry like that before. He really didn't know what to say, so he just apologized for starting shit. Nicholas accepted his apology, tapping fists with his old friend to signify that there were no hard feelings. Nicholas felt horrible for snapping at Jimmy like that.

Lynn was actually a beautiful Spanish model in a magazine that he had under his mattress. The fifty-two-page layout had various females displayed, but Lynn was the one that captured Nicholas's deepest interests. Her picture was quite exotic. Each of her curves was perfectly sculpted, creating a woman that fit Nicholas's ultimate desires as a teenage man. A well-exercised, dark-skinned angel was the only way to describe her. She had long, black, silky hair that reached clear down to the curve of her lower back. Nothing about this woman was disproportionate. And then there were her full juicy lips and alluring eyes. Some photos revealed her smile, a smile that would keep a man up at night if it was directed toward him. The magazine girl named

Lynn also matched the description of the shadow girl who occasionally danced across Nicholas's wall.

In the distance Nick and Jim could hear the sewer water splashing around violently as if someone was swimming or drowning. They moved faster, attempting to focus the lights from their miner's hats in the direction of the sound. The sound then stopped, as if they'd never heard it. They slowed their pace until they were just sliding their feet across the sewer floor. Nicholas then put out his long arm in front of Jim, stopping him completely. He pointed into the darkness at a figure heading toward them, a figure that resembled a man. Both boys held their position in the murky water, manning their sticks as if they were sharpened spears. When Jim's light fell on the man's face, they saw that his left eye was hanging on his cheek, dangling from the socket that it had been torn from. The man was so close that Nicholas could almost reach out and touch him. Then, out of the darkness, the man seemed to be dragged back, as if two men had hold of each of his arms. But no one could be seen. Nicholas ran toward the man as quickly as he possibly could.

The man was being pulled backwards at an abnormally fast rate, considering the level of the water they were all submerged in and the fact that there was nobody dragging him. Jim was running in the opposite direction, back toward the ladder, and was splashing wildly and making a panic-stricken commotion. Nicholas knew this had something to do with the shadows. He lowered his stick for battle and turned his pulse-pounding fear into courageous rage. Deep from within him came a roar that was so bold, it immediately transformed Jim's fear into heroic energy. Jim had assumed that Nick was right behind him, but when he saw that he wasn't, he immediately joined his friend to face the uncertain and the unknown.

Nicholas could see the man being lifted completely out of the water and slammed onto the elevated ledge ahead. The victim's voice screeched as if he hadn't spoken in years. Each word forced through his vocal chords was shrill and raspy. The echoes bounced from wall to wall and ceiling to floor. "Shut the lights! Shut the lights. Shut the lights!" The voice pierced the boys' ears. What Nicholas saw next scared him more deeply than anything he could have conceived. The wall in front of him illuminated by the light of his miner's hat was full of shadows. Shadows, ranging in all shapes and sizes, were watching a mortal man being murdered like it was a petty crime on a street corner. Jimmy caught up to Nicholas. His light was off, at the request of the screaming man who was being strangled while lying there alone.

Nicholas's light remained on, however, as he stood mesmerized by what the wall had to offer. Jim, on the other hand, did not see the shadows on the wall. What he did see were unexplainable events leading to a gruesome murder performed by invisible killers. Jim ran to the man's aid, not sure if what was attacking him would retaliate against him. As he drew closer, he could see that the man was living on borrowed time. Both of his ears were missing, as well as his eye. The rest of him was soaked with blood, and his legs had multiple breaks. The bone was even exposed through his pants in one place.

Jim yelled back to Nicholas but was unable to make contact, even though he was only a few yards away. Nicholas was not ignoring Jim, but he was temporarily unresponsive. Nick's face was white with fear as he continued staring at the wall. The sewer wall had nothing near it or on it as far as Jim could see, but Jim wasn't looking through Nicholas's eyes.

Jim then screamed again at Nicholas. "What's the matter with you? Are you crazy? Help me with this man!"

Nick turned his head to look at Jim. The light went out on his miner's helmet, so he took it off and slapped it with the palm of his hand until the light came back on. The wall before him was now empty, devoid of shadows, devoid of proof.

The boys attempted to help the man. He was almost dead. While holding him in their arms, they struggled to decide how best to treat his wounds with the limited resources they had and with no medical background. Judging by his appearance, they thought he was possibly a homeless man that lived in the sewer. He smelled as if he hadn't showered in months. The injuries were external and internal. One of his ears had been ripped off with such force that the flesh was torn clean to the edge of his mouth. Blood was flowing from his leg wounds and over a dozen puncture points across his old body. Nothing that Dr. Reid Anderson had taught could have prepared Nicholas for what he saw tonight. Nicholas was concerned with how Jim was going to cope with this experience and the many nightmares it might cause.

During this dreary moment in their history, three more shadows emerged on the wall. These shadows watched Nick and Jim and just stood there, proudly observing their devilish work. Leaving Jim with the man, Nicholas stood up and called them cowards. He waved his fists in the air, but they did not respond. Jim watched Nicholas. He felt the old man's body go limp as he whispered his last words. Jim was squatting down in the sewage, holding the man as if he was spending time with his own father on his deathbed during his final moments.

Nicholas was acting totally insane in the empty sewer. As Jim observed his actions, he was at a complete loss for words. This behavior went on for as long as Jim could stand it. His attempts to get Nick's attention were unsuccessful. Eventually he covered the homeless man with his sewer-sloshing raincoat. He then grabbed Nicholas by the collar of his jacket and forcefully tried to snap him out of his daze. Jim's quick snatch caught Nicholas off guard and sat his ass down in the dirty water. But Nick jumped right up and pushed Jim back.

Jim screamed in his face. "I'm leaving. One man is already dead, while you stare and yell at friggin' walls in the darkness." Jim headed back toward the ladder leading to the ground above.

Nicholas's ranting ended as he watched his concerned friend walk away. Suddenly a fourth shadow appeared on a short side wall where the sewer slightly slanted. It was Lynn. She stood there pointing to her right and directing Nicholas to shine his light on the other wall, where the shadow spectators from earlier had reappeared. Some of the shadows had their hands clasped on top of their heads, while others had their hands on their hips. A few appeared to be pacing around or crouching down. This behavior seemed to indicate that they did not condone the murder of the homeless man. On the contrary, they appeared to be concerned. Nicholas now understood that not all shadows are ill-intentioned when they try to make contact with the living. Some shadows are evil and have the ability to kill, while others reach out for help. Most simply exist in a world that can be seen by certain humans but not others. He walked toward the wall where Lynn's shadow was cast and thanked her for the message. She did not speak to him or make a sound. She only nodded her head to accept his thank you and then disappeared as she had done so many times before.

Upon her disappearance, the light on Nicholas's helmet once again went dark. Only this time it didn't matter how many times he slapped it around, it wasn't coming back on. Nicholas walked over to the deceased man to pay his last respects, then he headed in the direction of the ladder. While en route he could see that Jim was waiting for him at the bottom. Jim may have walked away irritated, but he'd never leave Nicholas alone in the dark. When Nicholas caught up with him, he could see that Jim had been crying. His eyes were red and teary, and he had puffy bags hanging underneath.

"Do you have any idea what the old man said to me prior to his death?" Jimmy asked Nicholas.

Nicholas shook his head. "No, I don't, Jim." He then asked, in a low voice, "What did he say?"

Jim explained the old man's interpretation of the shadows. "He started by telling me it doesn't matter how you've lived your life, either good or bad. The afterlife is undetermined until you get there. Shadows know that they're dead, but they don't understand why they can't rot in a box and be at peace. They can only be seen by chosen regulars. Regulars are people like you and me. The only difference is that some of us have the ability to see them.

Ghosts do not exist. When objects are moved or people think they see spirits, all they're seeing are shadows. Some shadows are violent, some are peaceful, but all are lost and depressed. Memories of their human lives are gone. All they know is that shadow life is forever, and forever is all they have."

As Jim climbed the ladder, Nicholas looked into the darkness one more time to see if Lynn was watching, but he saw nothing. Lynn and the other shadows were gone for the moment. Nicholas learned many lessons by visiting the sewer that day. He now knew that he wasn't alone, that he wasn't the only person tormented by shadows. The homeless man knew that fact as well. His new problem was going to be how to explain to his best friend the truth about things—his accident, the homeless man's death, or his love for a dead girl whom he'd never met.

On that night, or on any other night, Jimmy Meideros did not see a shadow. What he did see was a murder. But the murder they had witnessed could not be reported to the police. A helpless man had been killed by a supernatural force. And the man on his deathbed had said that eternal rest is a place where you possibly never sleep.

Shadow Chapter
NUMBER
Four...

Hours turned into days, while days became weeks, and eventually months gathered themselves into teams of twelve and changed their name to years. Time accumulates during good times and bad, without concern for weather or politics. People face a wide variety of situations throughout their lives, but it all happens under the hand of the unforgiving clock. As we struggle, the clock keeps ticking, despite our constant preoccupation with tracking time and slowing the process.

Nicholas considered the conventional methods of tracking time a nuisance. He did not have to mark progress by time in order to track success or accomplishments in life. Nick's life was not normal in the sense most people understand. As the years passed, Nicholas created his own calendar, which he called the "Habit Table." The Habit Table correlated months with shadow sightings and their behavior patterns. Nicholas knew that during the cold months, shadows were more likely to have the ability to grab solid objects, move items, and commit murder. In warmer weather, however, they were less active, and their behavior was more tolerable. Four years had passed since Nicholas and Jimmy witnessed the killing of the old man in the sewer. Jim took the man's death very hard, but despite witnessing the attack by unseen perpetrators, he was reluctant to repeat the tale to another living soul.

Nicholas was amazed by the energy that had flowed through the shadows during their supernatural attack on the homeless man. He was aware that a man was now dead. Nick also knew that according to the law, he and Jimmy could have been identified as accessories to murder for not having contacted the authorities immediately. Fortunately for them, no one knew that they had been there, and no evidence was found except for an old raincoat. Nicholas was able to use what he learned from that experience to further his own scientific research into the paranormal, research that he hoped would unlock the secrets of the shadows.

Nicholas wanted to do the right thing, out of respect for the deceased and to help soothe the conscience of his friend. Nick decided to ignore the conventional law system. The more he struggled with his internal turmoil, the more he realized Dr. Anderson's methods were working. Reid taught brilliantly. Nicholas, he said, had to face his fears and create permanent solutions. This simple statement sounds elementary, but how many people actually put the words into practice? Dr. Anderson supplied Nicholas with an arsenal of information. He allowed the kid to open his heart and unlock his brain. Nick wanted to become a weapon. He wanted to become a man who could survive on his own, with his common sense and clear-cut decisions. His future was going to be full of dangerous twists and turns. The shadows would remain a permanent part of his life, and they would control his every move unless he started controlling theirs first.

Oscar Gallo was the name of the man murdered in the sewer. His body was recovered a few weeks after Nick and Jimmy saw him last. Nicholas watched the whole thing on the six o'clock news. But after the incident took place, Nicholas was able to put the dead man on the back burner of his brain. He didn't want to dwell on negative events that were out of his hands. Nicholas often wondered how his old friend Jimmy Meideros was coping. Had he seen the man on the news and in the paper with his raincoat draped over him? Nicholas had every intention of discussing the event with Jimmy, but as we know, procrastination is difficult to spell but it's the easiest word to practice.

Nick and Jim did not speak to each other until many years later. In life, people come and go like passengers speeding by on a locomotive. The world is full of countless faces that will never have identities or names that we remember. Nicholas was sure, however, that his path would eventually cross Jimmy's in the future.

In the meantime his constant focus had to be shadow research and protecting his secret from his family. Understanding each of Reid Anderson's lessons would also come in handy. Nick sometimes felt like a Jedi knight from *Star Wars* who was under apprenticeship with Obi-Wan. He never told Reid about the shadows or that he had witnessed a murder in the sewer. Those things remained his secrets, but for some reason he felt Doc Anderson already knew.

By the age of fifteen, Nick had completed his entire high school education. Within that time he also had had hundreds of sessions with Dr. Anderson. These accomplishments were uplifting for Nicholas's parents. He was very proud that he could please them. At the same time he couldn't help but feel his time on earth was limited. We all live on borrowed time, no matter how old we are. How we spend our time is what matters.

Nicholas always tried to follow the rules that his parents wanted him to follow. But in his mind, he was developing a few rules of his own. He spent most of his time alone, for obvious reasons. Accepting additional people into his space seemed like more work than it was worth.

One day during his fifteenth year, Nick was lying in bed meditating. For him, meditation was more or less zoning out on the outskirts of sleep. He was struck with the notion that the man in the sewer might possibly have been mentally insane. If both the man and Nicholas had seen the shadows, why didn't they attack him too? Jimmy, in fact, had been more of a target than either of them, because he couldn't see anything. If they only attacked people who are already labeled nuts, that would protect the shadows from ever being discovered. No one would believe the stories, even if they were true.

Nicholas sat up in bed as if he had just discovered the cure for the common cold. He grabbed the phone book and began circling all the prisons and insane asylums in Rhode Island. He had a plan. He would visit each and every one of these institutions in hopes of possibly working with their outreach programs, if they had one. Maybe some of the inmates in these places weren't crazy at all, he thought. It's possible that they were victims of circumstance. Someone has to do the time for a crime. Nick thought that maybe it was time the shadows were brought into the light.

Nicholas began making phone calls in the name of shadow research. He felt a real sense of responsibility to find more people like himself. He was fortunate to have been blessed with a good upbringing and a positive support system. Not many people have great parents and a friend that's a psychiatrist to back them up and go to for advice. Reaching out to one single person would make his fight worth it, but Nicholas knew there had to be many more than one.

That evening Nicholas installed a lock on the inside of his bedroom door. Ever since he was eight years old, his parents had opened his door every night to check on him before bed. On the outside of the door he hung a note that said: "I love you guys, but a man sometimes needs his privacy." At the end of the note, he signed it "Love, Nicholas. See you in the morning." He also drew a smiley face to indicate everything was okay and not to worry. Nick's folks did stop by his room, and they did read the strange note. Believe it or not, they totally understood that a teenage boy needed his time alone for this and that. At that age, men and women undergo many changes, both physical and mental. Nicholas's parents cared for their son enough to respect his wishes and not disturb him. They never even knocked on the door.

The floorboards outside Nick's room were very squeaky. After Nicholas heard his parents walk in the opposite direction, he put his plan into action. First he hung blankets over the windows, firmly taping the edges and covering any spaces where light could enter his bedroom.

The room became so dark that it took almost five minutes for his eyes to adjust to the lightless cave he'd created. His room had a huge walk- in closet. Sleeping in there would ensure that he'd have no disturbances while he rested. The closet had no windows where shadows could catch the light that gave them their shape. Most evenings, he is awakened ten or more times throughout the night by strange sounds in his room. Sometimes door handles move on their own or things are knocked off of shelves or from the top of his nightstand. On other nights, it almost feels like someone is lying next to him, occupying the right side of his bed.

Reid Anderson had suggested the practice of "relocating" anytime Nicholas is awakened during sleep, in order to keep his body alert. Sleeping without any paranormal disturbance was uncommon for Nick, but then to relocate every time caused many restless nights. Normally Nicholas would follow Reid's instruction to the fullest detail, but tonight, rest was essential to his plan. Tomorrow he had a long day ahead of him. He'd be visiting many new destinations in search of the truth.

After he sprawled out on the wide floor in the dark closet, he remained undisturbed for nearly an hour. All of this extra drama in his life was actually a gift in disguise, Nicholas thought to himself. He felt that he was in fact chosen to be a savior of beings who were unable to help themselves. No matter what took place from this point forward, no matter what the risk, he was ready to accept what destiny had to offer. During that silent hour in the closet, Nicholas reflected on his life. His parents viewed his quiet demeanor as mature rather than odd. This meant they suspected that the incident that occurred when he was eight years old was an isolated event. They didn't have to be burdened with his problem. His secrets were sacred to him, and he would carry them alone till the end.

Over the last seven years, Nicholas figured he survived twenty-two attacks by shadows and avoided approximately fifty others. The torment that he endured would have mentally destroyed most people. But he remained humble, despite being harassed by faceless cowards. Even mafia bosses in charge of the biggest crime syndicates on earth don't dodge that many hits. Perhaps that is why Nicholas felt chosen and special.

Nicholas's closet was built with baseboard heaters. He thought it was very smart of the builders to be concerned about warm clothes. His house must have settled oddly after it was constructed, because the closet door didn't align properly when it was shut. The rest of the house was on a slight angle. If you placed a Matchbox car on the hardwood floor, it would roll clear to the other side of the room without being pushed. The gap in the door created a small passageway for air to enter the closet, and that alleviated the stuffiness while providing oxygen to breathe. Nicholas was now snuggled like a giant Swedish insect in his beat-up old type-two all-weather military-issue sleeping bag. The faded olive drab bag had seen better days. It remained musty even after it had been cleaned, and the zipper was broken, with sections torn right off, leaving only the snaps to secure it.

Before climbing into his cocoon, Nicholas sipped a capful of cough syrup to guarantee a silent night's rest. The syrup was working fast, but Nicholas still couldn't get to sleep. At night he was often filled with concern for his parents. That first night when he saw the shadow looking in at him through the living room blinds had left a frightening impression. When the same shadow appeared in his living room looking out from the blinds, the impression had become permanent. It was curious, Nicholas thought, that his parents never mentioned the bedrails mysteriously clanging in the hospital room. When he thought of it, it sent quivers down his spine. He assumed that it probably frightened them so much that it was easier to act as if it never happened. He was fairly certain that his parents had only heard the noise and not seen the shadow. But at this point, what did it matter?

His high level of brain activity combined with the nighttime cough syrup began to cloud Nick's already drowsy head. Past experience also taught him never to attempt solving problems when he was exhausted. Lying in the dark was the worst time to tackle issues that are best dealt with during the day. Nicholas released a long, deep yawn. The kind of yawn associated with at least eight hours of sleep. A yawn so deep and sleep inspiring that an insomniac would have been jealous. Nevertheless, Nicholas was wide awake. On one shoulder sat a small version of himself, telling him to follow his plan of action. On the other shoulder sat a small version of Dr. Anderson, telling him that since he's so comfortable and relaxed, he should go sleep somewhere else. Nick unsnapped the sleeping bag and sat up on the closet floor. He was exhausted, but he was going to relocate to the living room, if only to get Reid out of his head. Why would Reid be wrong now, Nicholas said to himself, as he rubbed his eyes and scratched his head?

Sleeping on the couch gave Nicholas a chance to check on his parents, which made him feel like a parent himself. He was curious if they had a lock on the inside of their door. Nicholas reached behind him to grab the police flashlight that Jimmy had given him on his birthday a few years ago. The flashlight was authentic. It even had a Providence Police Department sticker attached to the side of it. Nicholas thought that it would be rude to question where the gift came from, so he never did. He flipped the switch to the on position. The batteries must be getting old, he thought to himself, and maybe they came from the same package as the ones in his sewer sloshing miner's helmet. After a few more flips on and off, he was able to get a dim beam to shine on the once dark closet wall.

In front of him, a set of shadow arms emerged from the little light that was now present. They reached out and grabbed onto his ankles. He started to scream but then stopped himself so he wouldn't wake his parents. His skin was all pins and needles from head to toe as he watched the figure pull herself up like a swimmer exiting a pool. The patch of light that she cast herself in was only about as big as a trash can lid and certainly no larger than a hula hoop. Nicholas sat still on the floor, holding the flashlight in both hands as he concentrated on the female shadow in front of him. The startlingly tight grasp of her hands would not allow him to squirm away. As she pulled herself close to him, he kicked like a baby trying to free himself from its mother's womb.

Nicholas drew back his fist and was about to clobber the shadow when he realized that it was Lynn.

Near the end of the struggle, her silky locks whipped through the air as they had done when she danced on the hospital room wall. Nick tried to breathe in her beauty, but there was no odor other than that of his own fear-induced perspiration. He moved the flashlight closer to the wall in order to enhance her form and possibly see her more clearly. Nicholas was not scared anymore. He was no longer lost in amazement over Lynn grabbing his ankle. Now it was sheer astonishment over this incredible being allowing herself to be this vulnerable. Nicholas felt her release her grip. He was so close to her now that he could almost picture facial features. He envisioned the model Lynn as he'd described her to Jimmy years earlier. Her voluptuous, streamlined body was almost touching his.

She planted her hands flat on the floor, leaning in as if for a kiss. He caressed her hair while running his hand down her back. Her body had taken solid form, but Nicholas did not know for how long. She felt human, but Nicholas had never had contact with a human woman aside from his own mother. He imagined that this would be considered his first sexual encounter. Most men have the luxury of being able to kiss and tell to at least one living soul. How do you tell anyone that you had your first sexual experience with a gorgeous dead girl who happens to be a shadow? He didn't talk to too many people anyway. All he wanted was for the moment to never stop.

Lynn put her hand on Nicholas's cheek. They both leaned in, passionately engaging in a forbidden kiss, a kiss that Nicholas had dreamed about since the last time he saw her. If the circumstances of their brief meeting in the sewer had been different, maybe this encounter would have taken place sooner. He'd blocked the memory of the murder from his mind, leaving only one memory, that of exchanging glances with Lynn. Now, fortunately, he has two. Nicholas was so enveloped in his first supernaturally based sexual experience that he ignored his parents banging on his bedroom door. Almost simultaneously the kiss ended and the old flashlight batteries magically expired. Lynn vanished in a blink of an eye. She did, however, leave Nicholas with the first erection that wasn't the result of his own handiwork.

He stood up with some urgency and yelled "I'm coming" in response to his parents' knocking on his bedroom door. Afterward, he realized that was probably a bad choice of words for the current situation. Either way, his excitement dissipated pretty quickly when he thought about the kind of trouble he was in for not answering the door sooner. They banged so hard it shook the closet door. Nicholas did remember feeling a slight vibration during the kiss with Lynn. He thought that it was the earth moving, so to speak. Now he knew otherwise. While he fumbled for the key in his pocket, he couldn't think of a legitimate excuse. Once he opened the door, he expected the worst, but the hallway was empty. His parents were nowhere to be found. With his heart pounding, he raced down the hall to his mom and dad's bedroom. As Nicholas turned the corner, he slipped on their small throw rug, flipping the light switch on in the process. His parents were lying peacefully in bed. They looked as if they were sleeping, but as Nicholas drew closer he could see that they weren't. They were dead, murdered in their sleep.

He knew instantly that they'd been killed by shadows, innocent people suffocated while asleep in their beds. Nicholas stood there, weeping uncontrollably, tears running down his face. He was not at all responsible for their deaths, but he felt guilty just the same. All that he could think of was that his hesitation had killed them. If only he'd responded to their knocking, he thought if only …

Nicholas had tried so hard to follow Dr. Anderson's instructions that he had ignored the obvious. He'd ignored the fact that if he saw shadows, there was the extreme possibility that his parents may have too. Instead of openly addressing the attacks, the man in the sewer, and countless sightings, he'd said nothing at all. He truly thought he was protecting his family by keeping them in the dark.

He held his parents close for the entire night. In the morning, he contacted the authorities and told them what he had found.

Shadow Chapter
NUMBER
Five...

Nicholas hung up the phone after dialing the police. He still couldn't believe it. Even hours later when he again held his dead parents' hands one last time, he was in disbelief. While he sat there with them, he couldn't help but think of how they had held his hand when he lay injured in the hospital. They had always been by his side no matter what choices he made, good or bad. He regretted that he didn't say good night to them the evening before.

Even though they were already gone, Nicholas told his folks how much he loved them. During their last moments together, he also apologized for not communicating more about his involvement with the shadows. Dealing with this complicated problem by himself had made him feel in control of the situation. He'd thought if he could confine it all to his life alone, nobody else would be affected. Not in a million years did he ever imagine a tragedy like this would take place. Nicholas laid their hands across their chests and pulled the blanket over their heads. Before he left their bedroom to meet the authorities at the door, he made a promise to them. Nicholas promised to live a good life and become a man they could be proud of. He remembered Jimmy telling him how the homeless man in the sewer explained death, that humans had no souls when they pass. He'd said "either a shadow or rot in a box."

Nicholas knew that the shadows were real, but he had no proof that souls didn't exist. Before heading to the front door, he went back to his bedroom, where he dressed and gathered his personal belongings. In his bedroom closet he found what had to be a symbol displayed for his eyes only. The cord to his tape player was placed delicately on the floor next to his sleeping bag in the shape of a heart. Nicholas stared at the lovely design, somewhat comforted by the knowledge that even though he was now alone in this world, he was loved.

He put his belongings into an old gym bag and headed down the hall. As soon as he opened the front door, the police arrived on the scene. It was like something off of *Hill Street Blues*. Nicholas was met by three police officers and two plainclothes detectives. The detectives introduced themselves as Reilly and Arbor.

Detective Reilly was a very soft-spoken man who could get his point across without raising his voice. He was between thirty-five and forty years old and wore a military-style haircut, high and tight. The sides were shaved so closely, they must've been done with a straight edge blade. His pants and dress shirt were crisply pressed with well-defined creases. It appeared that he polished his own dress shoes like a soldier preparing for an inspection. His tie was plain black, complimenting his belt and the top portion of his hair that wasn't shaved. The detective's eyes were as blue as Dr. Chenker's back at the hospital, but without a creepy aura about them.

Detective Arbor was younger, perhaps twenty-three to twenty-five years old. He sported a similar haircut. Nicholas imagined that in a busy career like police work, hair that was easy to manage would mean less stuff to worry about when on a case or in a rush chasing criminals around town. He wore glasses, which he pushed up with his right index finger quite frequently. The frames were oval-shaped; the color appeared to be a light brown. Both men had similar build. Since Nicholas, who was a little over six foot, could see clear over both of their heads, he estimated they stood around five foot eight.

Detective Reilly was the lead detective on the case. Nicholas never asked for verification of this, but Reilly was older, and it seemed that Arbor nodded his head a lot and took notes as Reilly spoke. He entered facts into a small pocket notebook. Within minutes, the entire house was filled with police, ambulance personnel, and still more police. Detective Reilly asked Nicholas to sit down and explain every detail from the moment he found his parents. It seemed that Reilly wanted to get Nicholas's take on the situation before he heard the other detective's point of view.

Both detectives listened intently, neither interrupting Nicholas nor showing signs of disbelief as he related his extremely detailed story. Nick kept the story brief but informative and descriptive. The stuff about him and a shadow girl in the closet was under lock and key. If these guys showed up with twenty police cars, ambulances, and recently two fire trucks, there had to be a loony wagon somewhere. Nicholas was obviously in shock. He used that fact well as he explained what happened, exposing tears and sadness as he spoke. Each statement was elaborate, but formulated so that it would be easy for him to remember it later on when he'd be asked to repeat it. Inside, Nicholas desperately wanted to tell the exact truth about his parents' fate and that of the man in the sewer. Facts like that would send him straight to the electric chair, he thought. And despite their professional introduction, Nick had no idea who detectives Reilly and Arbor were. Trust is a thing that has to be earned over a long period of time, not by the flash of a badge. Even that statement seemed profound to Nicholas: they never even flashed a badge!

The entire truth, from soup to nuts, would be exposed once Nicholas could prove that shadows existed. He needed to obtain hard evidence, now more than ever, if he wanted to expose their existence to the entire world. Nicholas wanted vengeance, and vengeance is sometimes best achieved through patience. He felt he'd given the detectives all the information they needed to know in order to complete their investigation. All the other facts in his head were collected from years of torment, compliments of the shadows.

Detective Reilly asked Nicholas if he had any relatives that he could notify. Nick remained quiet, almost as if Reilly asked a trick question. The hair on the back of his neck was standing straight up. He immediately thought of Dr. Anderson, whom he regarded as next of kin. That notion sounded fine to Nicholas, but then again, Reid was not family and, to top it off, he was a psychiatrist. Nick was afraid that if the cops knew he saw a psychiatrist, they would blame this murder on him, thinking he's nuts. Lowering his eyes, Nicholas broke the silence by clearing his throat and then responded, saying that he had no other family members in America.

Both detectives made a mental note of Nicholas's response, and Arbor made an annotation on his clipboard. Nicholas tried not to appear nervous in front of the men, but his mind was racing a mile a minute. He then blurted out a request to use the bathroom. Asking for permission to use his own bathroom was the strangest request Nicholas had ever made in his entire life. The way things were going, though, made this seem like it was just the beginning of the road. Detective Reilly said, "By all means." He even apologized for not asking sooner. Considering the seriousness of the current circumstances, Nicholas felt better asking to use the bathroom rather than just walking away. For all he knew, they'd probably shoot him or cuff him for attempting to run. When Nicholas left the room, Reilly and Arbor entered the parents' bedroom to examine the scene.

Nick locked the bathroom door behind him and proceeded to vomit into the toilet. He heaved with so much force that he toppled over onto the floor from the effort exerted. Vomit ran down his cheek and dripped onto his shirt. As he hung on to the bathtub and toilet together, he looked at his distorted reflection in the bathtub faucet. Without realizing it, he was again using focal points. Staring at himself in a blurry amusement park mirror of sorts allowed him to pull it together. He forced himself to stand, grabbing onto any shred of hope that he had left in his soul. Pulling himself to the sink, he cleaned off his face then dried it on the towel. Behind him, the water dripped in the bathtub, one slow, methodical drop at a time.

Nicholas imagined how hard life must've been for his ancestors way back when. They had no running water, no heat, no electricity, and no supermarkets or malls to shop at. His thoughts were on the brink of delusion when suddenly the doorknob to the bathroom shook violently. Nicholas did not respond immediately. He held onto the sink as a support and considered whether he had more vomit to donate while the toilet was still close at hand. The rattling of the door handle came from Detective Arbor. After trying the handle and banging three times on the door, he asked if everything was okay. Nick replied, "I'm fine ... be out in a minute." He flushed the toilet, wiping away any residue on the rim, and headed out to face the music once again.

The front door to the house was open wide, exposing the entire lawn for Nicholas to see. There wasn't a vacant spot anywhere on the grass, with all the peeping neighbors and a swarm of strangers wishing to see the show. Everyone out there looked shocked and appalled. The crowd gasped as Nicholas's parents were wheeled out in body bags one after the other. Detective Reilly walked up to Nicholas in the living room to inform him that his parents had in fact been suffocated simultaneously, but they didn't suffer due to the fact that they were asleep when it took place. Nicholas never turned his head to acknowledge the man; he just stared blankly at all the people on the grass outside. Reilly patted him on the shoulder and told him he was very sorry for his loss.

The word simultaneous meant shadows to Nicholas. Reilly or Arbor never mentioned the words "break-in" or "intruder" in regards to the culprits. It seemed that there was something they were not revealing. A murder with no motive, no suspects, and no questions about suspicious characters was unheard of. If no questions were asked, then more information must already be known. Nicholas was now weary of everyone around him, both living and dead.

Mr. and Mrs. Johansson's corpses were loaded up and taken away like a couple pieces of old furniture being sold at an auction. The people on the grass began leaving the scene now. Some had their arms around each other, and others had placed their hands on their hips or were scratching their heads as they walked off. As horrible as Nicholas felt at the moment, the scene outside of his house struck him as strangely humorous. These people were reacting to his parents' death just like the shadows who watched the murder in the sewer. There were only a few striking differences. These people were alive, of course. And in the sewer, nobody acted as if they saw each other, nor did they comfort one another. It was almost as if they could see the humans, but not the other shadows. If this was true, then Lynn was definitely different.

Nicholas went in the other room and sat on a rocking chair. The cushions on it were stuffed with wool from a sheep farm in Sweden. He remembered back when he was four or five years old. He used to take those cushions and tie the strings together to create body armor. Once the strings were tied tight, he would stick his head through the middle and pretend that he was a Viking. Then he would pillage the kitchen cabinets, looking for Twinkies and Ring Dings. And his father would cry out, "Help us. It's Nicholas the Viking!" His mom would get mad at his dad for egging him on, but now that he looks back at it, he thought that she was acting a little bit too.

Detectives Reilly and Arbor entered the room where Nicholas was sitting in the rocking chair. They asked him if he knew a Dr. Reid Anderson. Nicholas did not hesitate for a second. He informed the detectives that Reid was his psychiatrist and one of his best friends. Detective Reilly smiled at Nicholas, mentioning that Reid was the finest child doctor in the state of Rhode Island. He also went on to say that he was happy that Nicholas would have the opportunity to continue working with Reid, despite the nature of the circumstances. Detective Arbor handed Nick two business cards. One card had Reilly's information on it, and the other had his own. They informed Nick that he could call the numbers on the cards at any time and that they were at his disposal twenty-four hours a day, seven days a week. Arbor also shook Nick's hand and extended his sympathy for his great loss, as Reilly had done earlier. The two men then excused themselves and headed out the open front door.

Nicholas was now an island. He was a single being alone in this world. All he had were his thoughts and his shadow, and a shadow of some dead chick that he didn't quite understand. Loneliness was never this bad, because he knew that his parents were only down the hall. Now it was time to be a man.

Nicholas underwent many life-altering changes when the shadows entered his world, complicating even the simplest of things. Change is a definite part of life, and death is an inevitable change that happens to us all. Nicholas loved his parents with all of his heart, and he wished that he was dead instead of them. His wish would never be granted, but he was sure he could fulfill his promise to carry on the Johansson name. Their good name would not be tarnished by this tragedy, nor would accusations be made about their only son murdering them in cold blood. Maybe when he was a kid, his father was planting a seed by referring to him as a Viking. The Vikings were explorers who accidentally discovered a new world. Nicholas, at that very moment, named the new world that he discovered: he called it "the shadow life."

A woman's voice called Nicholas's name from the kitchen. He slowly walked in there, not sure who he was going to see. Lynn had never spoken to him before, he thought to himself. Possibly it was her in her shadow bathrobe and slippers, offering him a cup of coffee and a bagel. As strange as that notion sounds, is it any stranger than anything else Nicholas had seen lately? When he entered the room, there was a woman standing there to greet him, and she wasn't a shadow. She reached out her hand, introducing herself as Donna McClennon. Without sounding fake, she offered her condolences to Nicholas. He really liked her right from the start. Her face was very genuine and friendly. She reminded him of somebody, but he couldn't put his finger on exactly who. During her introduction, she explained that she was a social worker who would be assisting him with a place to live, since he was a minor.

Donna wore her brown hair in a bun supported by a large rubber band. She was about forty-five years old and stood around five and a half feet tall. Her attire was very casual but at the same time professionally chosen to compliment her line of work as a social worker dealing with kids. Nicholas picked up his belongings and followed the woman out the side door. There was no reason to lock the front door, for there were still a few policemen and women inside doing whatever it is they do in a situation like this.

She drove a small pickup truck that didn't have government plates attached. Donna watched Nick's eyes observe the plates before he got in the passenger's side. She then smiled and said to him, "I drive my own truck because I can smoke in it." Nicholas just smiled at her and sat down inside. He was feeling the effects of the situation very heavily at the moment. Before she started the engine she asked, "Do you mind if I light up a cigarette?"

"Not at all," Nicholas replied. "Can I have one?"

"Yes, as soon as I break your fingers," Donna said. She then smiled another friendly grin and started the engine, looking both ways before she pulled out. Nicholas gave her a slightly confused glance, wondering if she was serious but hoping that she wasn't. Donna quickly cleared the air. "Sorry," she said, "I have an odd sense of humor."

Nicholas smiled. "Lately, mine is too, so thanks for the laugh. I needed one. So, where are we going?"

"We're heading to the House of Young Hearts."

The ride to the state's orphanage and youth facility was very quiet. Nicholas was in deep thought, wondering if the two shadows in the sewer had killed his mom and dad. Was Lynn in on it as a distraction? To conclude that there could only have been two killers would be ridiculous. If there were two, then there could be two hundred or two thousand or two million. Rhode Island is the smallest state in the country, Nicholas thought to himself. Imagine how many shadows there were in Texas. Nicholas tried to block the negative thoughts from his mind, as he felt all the bumps in the road in Donna's tiny truck. The pleasant thought that he focused on was Lynn in his closet. He didn't want to rule her out as a suspect, but at the same time, she couldn't have been involved in the murder. He had to believe that the heart symbol she left on the floor in his closet represented her love toward him. Even as smart and strong as Nicholas was, he was still a teenage Viking boy in love.

On the evening of Nicholas's gruesome discovery, he had made plans the next day to investigate insane asylums, prisons, and homeless shelters. He was going to attempt to get answers to questions, answers that would explain the unexplainable. There are people out there who are wrongly accused of crimes and live as prisoners each and every day. These people are forced to live in complete and total grief as a result of evil. That same evil knew of Nicholas's plans and temporarily stopped him from carrying them out.

In the forty-five minutes it took them to reach the orphanage, they had traveled almost the entire length of the state of Rhode Island. They were in southern end of the state on the border of Connecticut. Donna parked her vehicle in a spot next to an old tree. The tree didn't have very many branches, but those it did have were long and twisted, supported by a narrow trunk. The roots shot out of the base like lava down the side of an angry volcano. Nicholas examined the tree from the passenger's window while waiting for Donna to bark an order at him in her sarcastic way. Donna did the complete opposite of what Nicholas expected. She applied the emergency brake then placed her right hand over Nicholas's left hand, squeezing it gently. She positioned herself sideways in her driver's seat facing Nicholas. Donna looked as comfortable as a person would be sitting on their couch at home. When Nicholas looked over at Donna, she had a tear forming in her right eye, as if her grief was for someone that was close to her.

"Why are you crying?" he asked.

"I was friends with your mom and dad back when we were kids in high school. You know, the world is very unfortunate to have lost a couple as special as your parents."

Nicholas thanked her for her beautiful sentiments while trying to fight back his own tears. He raised his left hand, kissing the top of hers, and then opened his door and began walking toward his temporary home.

Donna gave herself a moment to compose herself, wiping away her tears. She was amazed by the maturity of Nicholas. He had definitely been raised by the two that she remembered from back when she wasn't much older than he is now. Donna stepped out of the car and walked with Nicholas up the long cobblestone trail to the front doors of "The House of Young Hearts."

Nicholas held the door for Donna as they entered the old stone building. Once inside, they walked through a dimly lit corridor to a window with a sign that read "Welcome. Please ring for service." Donna tapped the bell once, but before she could blink, a familiar voice from behind her asked, "May I help you?" Nick and Donna spun around and were comfortably greeted by none other than Dr. Reid Anderson himself. Nicholas's face lit up for the first time since he kissed his shadow princess Lynn. Instead of shaking Nicholas's hand, the doctor embraced him like a son and offered his condolences.

Nicholas attempted to introduce Donna McClennon to Reid Anderson in an effort to be polite to his new friend. Donna laughed and hugged Reid very tightly. Nick didn't know what to say, so he stood silently, waiting for one of them to speak. Donna looked back at Nicholas with one arm still around Reid and said, "Maybe I should introduce you to someone."

Nicholas played the game and asked the silly question. "Who?" He knew it was obviously Reid, but he asked anyway.

She smiled from ear to ear and proudly said, "My son, Dr. Reid Anderson."

Reid looked incredibly proud to hear his mother say those words. He explained that Donna had adopted him from this very facility when he was only eight months old. She was also kind enough to let him keep his birth name so that he could carry on his family name. Reid's story brought hope to Nicholas's heart. He had just lost both parents, but now it seemed he had gained two lifelong friends.

The three stood in that spot in front of the counter, enjoying what they had together. As they stood there, the small bell in the office rang behind them, just as it had when Donna tapped it. But this time there was no one there. They had expected someone to be standing ready to greet them. And yet the small bell on the dusty ledge had apparently managed to ring all by itself. It was very unsettling. Nicholas felt cold fear trickling all over his body, as if ice water had been poured over his head when he least expected it. He looked around the room but saw no shadows. Nick knew from his many years of unfortunate experience that shadows don't have to show themselves to be watching.

Reid placed his hand firmly on Nicholas's shoulder. Donna once again held his hand tightly. Reid stepped forward and said, "Nicholas, you're doing fine. You're winning the battle."

"What battle am I winning?" Nicholas replied. "I just lost my parents."

Reid whispered to him so Donna couldn't hear. "You have succeeded, Nicholas, where I failed."

Nicholas stepped backwards as if Reid's words had scared him. His eyes opened wide and his jaw dropped in shock. "You knew!" Nicholas muttered, "you knew!"

The lady behind the reception counter then decided to show up, greeting the three with a shrill voice. "May I help you?"

Shadow Chapter
NUMBER
Six...

Processing the initial paperwork to get into the House of Young Hearts took far less time than Nicholas had anticipated. Reid and Donna basically took care of the majority of the forms, most of which pertained to their profession and connection with the boy. Nick was asked a few questions here and there and was forced to fill out a long, drawn-out survey, which had questions about feelings and all kinds of other crap that Nicholas didn't care to think about at the moment.

While this office business took place, Nicholas remained puzzled about why Dr. Anderson had never discussed his shadows. He'd also been caught off guard when he learned that Donna was Reid's mom. Despite the small missing bits of information, Nick still trusted Reid greatly. He had his own secrets, too, that he kept quiet about. Seeing shadows is a pretty big secret, and being in love with one is even bigger. Anything is possible in this screwed up world, Nicholas thought to himself. There was another question bouncing off the walls in his teenage brain: What if Donna and the detectives could see shadows? Donna would never tell Reid's secret, and if Reilly is truly Reid's buddy, he wouldn't tell anyone either. Maybe they're all involved in a small shadow cult and are thinking of conducting an initiation to see if the young Viking was worthy of joining the club.

One possibility led to another in Nicholas's mind. Where do you draw the line when weighing all the what-if 's? A line had to be drawn somewhere if you were going to decide whom to trust and whom not to trust. Nick had heard Reid let the cat out of the bag with his own two ears. The best thing to do now was react carefully to all conversation. Having a good understanding of what level these people were on would dictate whether they would become lifelong allies.

He carefully watched as mother and son expertly sorted through his newly created file. Their close attention to detail was comparable to his mother's. The school lessons that she prepared for him and her incredible teaching techniques had allowed him to complete his high school education three years ahead of schedule. She was a stickler when it came to attention to detail, right down to remembering to dot the i's. Reid and Donna did in fact share countless qualities that reminded him of his mother and father. Observing them made Nicholas think that Reid may have withheld his knowledge of shadows for a good reason. The young man would never have doubts about these people again. His heart told him that they were here for a reason and the reason was a good one.

Nicholas dreaded the upcoming week at his new home. He kept picturing how sad and dismal the funeral would be. Life can change in a blink of an eye, without hesitation and, worst of all, without notification. Maybe, he thought if tragic events came equipped with early detection kits, like prostate exams, sickness and death would be easier to deal with. Imagine what would happen if we could foresee car accidents, heart attacks, or earthquakes. Our world would be overpopulated, and as a civilization we would run out of land to live on or food to eat. Avoiding the Grim Reaper a few times in life is luck. The best thing to do is be thankful for the good times. Good times don't last forever, but neither do bad times. Nicholas has rationalizing down to a science. The only problem is that the constant contradictions of his rationalizing tie his brain in knots. Time and maturity will have to iron out the wrinkles.

The woman at the counter, who's the shrill voice bespoke coffee drinking and cigarette smoking, wore an orange name tag on which her name was spelled out in bold, black letters: SUMMER. Though it was obviously legible enough to read, the letters were lopsided, sloppily stuck on with some kind of peel-off adhesive tape. Even at first glance Nicholas could see that she had been attractive at some point in her life, but she wore too much makeup and her clothing didn't look appropriate for an out-of-shape woman of her age. It seemed like she was the type of gal who for a hobby would stay up late binging on food. Nicholas wasn't passing judgment on this woman; he was just making another observation from a teenage point of view.

Nicholas had been sitting against the wall in an old wooden office chair with no wheels. He wasn't bothered that Summer hadn't introduced herself when he entered her office or after he'd sat there for twenty plus minutes. These places were well known for their inhospitable ways. If he was going to be categorized as a file with a number attached to it rather than as a person, that was fine by him. At least now he knew where he stood.

The office had no character. The décor must have dated back to the sixties. There was a small plaque on the wall that looked like an award next to her dirty unorganized desk. The plaque read "Summer Mahoney—proud employee for eleven years." Under her name was some kind of stamp signifying the approval of some authority. She obviously didn't care much for the award, because it was heavily tarnished and hanging crooked. Located about a foot under the award was a photo of three young boys, all with their arms around each other.

One was black, one was Hispanic, and the other was white. Nicholas assumed that the guys in the picture were residents at the home and lived somewhere in the building. He thought maybe they gave Summer the picture as a gift of some kind. Nicholas wasn't planning to ask Summer about the photo, but she blurted out from across the room, with a mouth full of food, "Do you like the picture?" Her Rhode Island accent didn't mix well with the cake and ice cream she'd crammed in her face.

"Yeah, it's nice," he replied. "Do they live here in this building?"

She swallowed her food and broke into a broad smile, exposing lipstick-smudged teeth and large, receding gums. "Those are my sons," she said. "They all have different daddies." Reid shot Nicholas a quick glance, raising his eyebrows at her comment. Donna grinned politely. Her smooth grin made Nicholas smile, but not in a way that would have hurt the woman's feelings if she happened to notice.

Nicholas was very mature for a teenage boy, but like all teenage boys, he labeled things certain ways, either literally or figuratively. Most teenage labels shouldn't be spoken aloud, so Nick kept this one private. He secretly called her "Summer Kids" instead of Summer Mahoney, since "some o' her kids" had this father, and some had another. Either way, it didn't matter. As long as she was a good mom and took care of them, who could ask for anything more. He felt bad afterwards for being so judgmental. If Summer had known of his situation with Lynn, she'd probably call him Ghost Boy or Shadow Boy or Shadow Lover or whatever.

Donna and Reid handed in all the documents to Summer once they were complete. Then Donna walked over to Nicholas to ask if he wanted to see his temporary residence. Donna had a way about her that could take the stress out of any situation.

Before Reid headed over to Nicholas, he spoke to Summer. "Thanks for accepting the boy on such a short notice. These troubled situations can be very drawn out when dealing with a minor. Nicholas had no blood relatives, so this place was the best choice for the meantime."

When Summer reached out to shake Reid's hand, Nicholas spied a black, heart-shaped locket hanging from a chain around her neck. It was a rather large pendant and seemed to have a slightly purplish cast to it. Nicholas jumped out of his chair and walked swiftly past Donna to get a closer look at the mysterious piece of jewelry. As he lunged toward her, Summer stepped backwards, not knowing what to expect. Her movements were rather awkward, and she accidentally bumped into her swivel chair in the process. "Nicholas," she asked, "what's wrong?"

Reid didn't even know what to say to this giant kid. Nick was always so laid back, so this behavior was slightly alarming to all who were in the room. Nick laid his giant hand on the desk and leaned in to ask a question. His eyes never left the locket, not even for a second. He pointed to the locket and asked, "Could I please hold your locket? It's quite beautiful." Summer nervously grinned and laughed a nervous, half laugh. As Donna slowly made her way over to them, she made eye contact with Reid. Reid nodded his head to assure his mother that all was fine. Nicholas asked another question. "Is there a picture inside of a beautiful Spanish girl, possibly between the ages of eighteen and twenty?" Summer collapsed into the chair behind her. The room was completely silent. Summer swallowed a few times. When she was finally able to speak, she replied to Nick's question in a high-pitched wail. "Yes! But how could you know?" Her face was so pale that Donna started to fan her with a piece of paper.

From where Nick, Reid, and Donna were standing, it appeared that the locket was suspended on a stick lying in the straight vertical line of Summer's cleavage; the locket on the stick looked almost like a lollipop. Summer was trying to pry it open with her yellow- and blue-painted fingernails. She tried to slip a nail beneath the cover of the locket, but the tiny clasp wouldn't budge. They waited patiently, watching as Summer fumbled around. Nicholas imagined the locket was Lynn's tiny heart-shaped casket. His mind must have been on tombs and graves at the moment to imagine such a thing. Perhaps his subconscious was trying to suppress the devastating thought of his parents' funeral for the moment. He continued to try and focus on the positive.

Summer finally opened the locket. She was so excited. It looked like she'd won the lottery. But her cheers ended when all the lights in the building suddenly shut off, leaving them in complete darkness. Summer's office was down a corridor devoid of windows. The only natural source of light was a skylight twelve feet above her desk. They heard an orchestrated snapping of switches around the building, killing the illumination everywhere. In all the rooms, curtains and shades were systematically closed, turning the orphanage into a lightless box of frenzy. Fire alarms roared and children screamed. The building seemed to come alive. Nicholas could feel that something horrible was about to take place. And unfortunately, it was something related to him.

In the dark office Nicholas heard a thud and a woman's scream only a few feet in front of where he was standing. Summer had been thrown from her chair and had landed face down on the linoleum, her nose broken. Her necklace was viciously ripped from her neck. The chain whipped across the delicate tissue of her neck, causing instant bleeding. Nicholas reached out into the dark, calling for Reid and Donna, but there was no answer. Nicholas got down on his hands and knees and crawled to where Summer had fallen. She was unconscious but breathing. As he placed his hand on her desk chair to move it out of the way so that he could tend to the woman's injuries, an unseen force unexpectedly dragged her from behind the desk and out the office door. The door swung open just long enough for her body to clear the opening. It then slammed shut, sealing Nicholas inside. During his panic, he imagined that Reid and Donna had exited the same way.

Many of the children at the House of Young Hearts had spent most of their lives in that building. During a crisis, the older children were expected to work alongside counselors to help get problems under control. They were assigned jobs like activating emergency lights and leading younger kids to safety and out of harm's way. The facility's plans for incidents like this were taught, practiced, and reinforced. There weren't many situations these kids weren't prepared for, and they were ready to act on a second's notice to save another person's life. Thirty-minute training drills were conducted sporadically three or more times a month at undisclosed times throughout the day and evening. The drills were conducted year-round, regardless of whether it was in the nineties or below zero. Children new to the facility occasionally had a hard time adjusting to the practice drills and the alarms, but after a while they realized it's for their own safety. During practice drills, the children form lines so that a head count can be calculated. Fire alarms sound different from alarms for natural disasters such as earthquakes, tornadoes, or hurricanes. Having the two different alarms sounds confusing, but different escape tactics came into play in the various scenarios.

Reid and Donna had been roughly dragged off and left on the hallway floor outside the office. Their abductors were apparently very strong and fast. The two were awake during the incident, but neither saw anybody touch them at all. These people had to have been hiding somewhere in the office the entire time—assuming they were even people. Summer was on the floor beside them, covered in blood but breathing steadily. She was incoherent, and her locket was gone. Reid helped Donna carry Summer out the front door of the building. As they passed a phone in the hallway, Reid ordered one of the older kids to call the police and tell them to bring an ambulance as soon as possible. Donna was frantic as hell, despite trying to keep her composure. As they carried Summer to safety, she yelled to her son, demanding to know what was happening and where Nicholas was. They carefully placed Summer on the ground in a safe location where she could wait until the paramedics arrived. Reid then ran back toward the building, desperately screaming Nicholas's name.

All the children in the House of Young Hearts made it safely out of the facility in record time and without injury. They sat outside of the building in the embrace of each other's arms. Most of the kids were crying, and many were trying to calm their friends. To say the least, they were all terrified by what had taken place in their home.

A power outage and forceful winds did not cause this to happen. Nobody tripped a circuit breaker or played a practical joke. Each of the children had seen the heavy windows crash to their sills. Curtains and blinds dropped by themselves, blocking all light from entering. Light switches clicked on and off in some rooms five or six times, as if manipulated by invisible fingers. The scariest part of their experience, however, was what they heard just before they evacuated the building. It was the sound of bare feet running around in every room. The sound of invisible feet slapping against the floor was enough to cause mass hysteria. Despite all their preparation for emergencies, there was no alarm to warn the children of something like this.

The heavy wooden door at the main entrance to the orphanage slammed shut after the last child came out. Reid and Donna pulled on the handle, but it wouldn't budge. They kicked the door and screamed Nicholas's name, but there was no answer. Donna screamed Nicholas's name repeatedly. And she begged Reid to tell her what was going on. Reid looked at his mother and told her to stay where she was and wait for the police to arrive. He said he was going to go around back and attempt to scale the building's maintenance ladder to the roof, and from there he could enter through the skylight in Summer's office. Donna had a very strong connection with her adopted son Reid. She could feel his need to shelter Nicholas from whatever was inside.

Everything Donna ever imagined about the supernatural was incorrect. She imagined they would be clothed, but the figures that dragged them from the office had been completely naked, just as the children said. Their hands were neither cold nor warm; they were merely tools which they clamped over their mouths so they wouldn't scream. Donna, too, remembered hearing their bare feet slap the floor. Although they never spoke a word or sighed, she could tell they weren't human.

In the distance, they heard the roar of sirens heading to the scene. Inside the office, another roar was heard, a roar that seemed to sound like a man. The echo was so powerful, it stunned the crowd outside and commanded the attention of every man, woman, and child. They rose to their feet like fans at a sporting event. Suddenly, from inside the walls of the home, Nicholas's deep voice thundered, demanding the truth. "Did you kill my family?" he screamed. "Are you responsible for my pain?" Over and over he asked these questions. "You faceless cowards," he shouted. Using his hate to conquer his fear, he said boldly, "I am alone, and I am not afraid to die."

Reid, unable to get on the roof, came around the other side of the building. He could hear Nicholas clear from the back of the building. No one could imagine what was taking place in the small sealed office. One of the kids asked Donna if the Incredible Hulk was in there. From the sound of the screams and smashing, he wasn't far off. Summer, meanwhile, was propped against a tree and being attended to by a paramedic who had just pulled up on the scene. One of the kids was holding her free hand, showing her that he was concerned.

When the bell in Summer's office rang all by itself, Nicholas had a feeling that something was going to happen. Now that he was in the midst of this situation, he knew that Lynn had rung the bell as a warning. While Reid and Donna filled out the paperwork, Nicholas was already scanning the room for weapons. Sticking out of the arm of the wooden chair that he was sitting in was a large rusty nail, which he quietly pried out, thinking he could use it between his knuckles as a spike if necessary. On Summer's desk he'd seen a pair of sharp scissors, and there was a mop in the corner of the room. He thought he might be able to use the thick black industrial rubber band that he always wore on his right wrist to bind the scissors to the mop handle and create a spear.

To the crowd outside, it sounded like World War III. Nicholas was outnumbered, but not alone. The first blow was a stiff jab to the ribs. That was followed by a heavy metal trash can slamming him in the head. Initially, he thought the abuse was tolerable, almost weak in comparison to what he imagined the supernatural should be capable of. It felt like there were dozens of them in the room. Like a group in a mosh pit at a rock concert, they were getting their licks in one by one, some more violent than others. Once they had Nicholas lying helpless on the floor, they began violently stomping his face and body from all directions. Then they held him down flat on the floor as if they were going to cut him open. His heart was pounding profusely, but his struggling was useless.

Suddenly Summer's desk began to shake, and it rose seven feet off the floor. Nicholas scrunched his face and tensed his body, waiting for the impact. The steel office desk filled with supplies directly hit Nicholas, but it affected him no worse than if he'd been hit by a pillow during a children's sleepover. Invisible feet ran in all directions in the dark office. They reluctantly released Nicholas when it appeared they were unable to kill him. A blow from a desk of that size and weight should have been lethal. Nicholas had apparently been blanketed from the attack by Lynn, who absorbed the majority of the blows. Because she was already dead, she could not feel physical pain or be killed, nor could she be disfigured or critically injured. Her body became one with his body, adding an impenetrable layer of defense against the shadows.

Nicholas stood up, brushing himself off. His eyes had adjusted to the darkness, and he could see that the office was destroyed. Now he realized that the shadow attacks in the past were never successful because Lynn was always there. When he slept, she was there, and when they were close by watching him, she was there. Now she was attempting something else. Lynn was going inside him. She stepped into his body, allowing him to feel her much more deeply than he'd felt her before. This new experience was even more fascinating than their time together in his closet. He could not read her exact thoughts, but he could sense her feelings as if they were his own. She cared deeply for him as a friend, and now appeared to be crossing the boundaries and falling in love. When she was inside, he could see through her eyes. The room was still filled with shadows, but they were tightly pressed against walls and hiding around corners. Through Lynn's eyes, they looked like ordinary shadows though they acted like criminals. Soon they all disappeared, hiding like the cowards that Nicholas knew they were.

Nicholas was now truly a Viking. He was a being of ultimate ability. In the past history of his family, there were great people, but never a man who walked among shadows. Had there been one, had there been a story as amazing as this, it would have become a legend, and his story would have been passed down through the generations.

His new discovery was truly unbelievable. He and Lynn would be able to battle the shadows, sending them back to the dark holes that they crawl out of. While Lynn was still inside of Nicholas and he could see through her eyes, he discovered that not all the shadows here were violent. A few were seated in corners of the room, scrunched into balls and appearing weak or depressed. He thought to himself that if Lynn was a good shadow, there must be more like her.

Nicholas hated the evil shadows. They were responsible for killing his parents as well as the homeless man in the sewer. From this day forward, he would refer to them as Rippers. Sad or depressed shadows, on the other hand, will be Dormants, and shadows who reached out to a human without intending harm would be called Faith Finders.

Nicholas wanted to help the Dormants that he saw around him, but he didn't know how just yet. If they didn't want violence, maybe they just wanted answers for why they were alone in the shadows. Even for a mortal living in the light, it's sometimes lonely. Other people's behavior can make you withdraw or feel singled out. Imagine a planet filled with billions of people like that.

Detectives Reilly and Arbor ran up the long patch of grass on the west side of the orphanage's lawn, accompanied by a large German shepherd named Lomax. Lomax had been trained by the two detectives from the time he was a puppy. Not only was the canine a perfect specimen, he was a member of the police department and had even been assigned a badge number. Around children he was as gentle as a kitten, but with a criminal in his sights he was a four-legged nightmare. When the three reached Reid and Donna, they were at a loss for words to explain what was taking place or how to deal with it.

Reilly immediately ordered a few of the local police standing by their cruisers to break the door down. But his order was quickly overruled by a big, lopsided local detective who called himself "the boss." After he cancelled Reilly's order, the boss slowly walked up to him and explained, in a belittling manner, why he'd been given that nickname. The man seemed to rapidly grow in height as he drew closer. But Reilly and Arbor held their ground as the large detective launched into a time-wasting explanation. Reilly, a complete gentleman and total professional, gave the ignorant man a considerate thirty seconds, but at the end of his spiel, Reilly reissued his order to break the door down. The local detective, however, showed no concern or compassion for Nicholas Johansson's well- being and instead started ranting and raving about his jurisdiction in this matter. He then made the hugely drastic mistake of pointing his chubby finger in the smaller detective's face and stepping closer to emphasize his useless opinion by tapping the left side of Reilly's chest.

The calm collective detective winked at his four associates to indicate that they should step aside. Young Detective Arbor had been present in the past when Reilly had to give someone an attitude adjustment. It was always very neat and polite but at the same time painful and very effective. Arbor reached in front of Reid and Donna and guided them a few steps back, out of harm's way. Lomax sat down like a good boy and watched the spectacle patiently, never once growling. Had Reilly called his name for assistance, it would have been a different story, and the show would have ended very quickly. But Reilly could deal with it himself. A direct thrust with a straight right palm to the forehead jerked the giant imbecile's head backwards and rocked him up on his heels. Reilly snatched the officer's fat arm in a twisting wrist lock and lowered his arrogant carcass to the ground in one swift move. The entire process of getting the man's attention took only a matter of seconds. Detective Reilly was now able once again to direct the police officers to use the ram to knock the door in and bring Nicholas to safety.

At Reilly's insistence, the boss, whose real name was Alistair Butterbyne, quickly apologized to Donna for any obscenities he may have muttered. On his knees, Butterbyne no longer appeared very massive. His twisted hand was now slightly red and on the verge of turning purple. Detective Reilly then requested that Arbor take Reid, Donna, and Lomax closer to the building to wait for Nicholas to exit. Turning the fat detective's wrist one more click was all Reilly had to do in order to see him sweat like a pig.

After Donna was out of earshot, he bent down and whispered directly in Detective Butterbyne's ear. "Listen here, bub, I'm a sergeant first class in the Army National Guard." He pointed to the location of where his Combat Infantry Badge he earned during Desert Storm would be worn if he was in military uniform. "The Combat Infantry Badge is a badge that real men sometimes die trying to earn. And mark this, when it comes to Nicholas Johansson, no matter if it's in Rhode Island, Sweden, Kuwait, or friggin' China, he's in my jurisdiction." The man nodded to express that he understood. As he was released, he fell to the ground.

Before the police could force the door to The House of Young Hearts off its hinges, Nicholas opened it and stepped out. The fresh air had never felt so exhilarating. He could feel his beautiful bulletproof vest separate herself from him, blending back into the shadows. Nicholas announced the all-clear. Everyone was very happy to see him safe, but they were confused at the same time. Donna ran to Nicholas, hugging him as if he had been missing for a year. She put her hands on his cheeks and stared him in the eyes. "What the hell happened in there?" she asked. He just smiled and hugged her back. Over Donna's left shoulder, Nicholas reached out to Reid with an offering clenched in his fist. Reid put out his hand to receive the black, heart-shaped locket that had been ripped from Summer's neck during the attack. The locket opened much more easily this time. Inside was exactly what Nicholas had guessed. The photo was actually more beautiful than the model he'd named Lynn after. Reid stared at the picture for a brief moment. He then asked Nicholas if this girl had been a friend of his.

Before Nicholas could respond, the group's attention was diverted by Lomax, who was lying on his back in the grass beside the building, within the slightly angled shadow cast by the side of the cement staircase. Though the dog appeared to be comfortable, he was letting out a slight soothing howl under his breath. The two detectives quickly noticed the howl and moved in closer to investigate. Reilly walked up to him and snapped his fingers three times. Three snaps normally would direct the animal to come to his master and sit directly in front of him waiting for his next order. But Lomax did not respond in any way, shape, or form. Arbor then called his name in a stern voice, ordering him to obey, but still there was no response. This dog had never ignored an order from Reilly or Arbor. He was a trained professional, bred for obedience and loyal beyond any standard a human could possibly imagine. Astounded, the two men stood there looking back and forth at each other and at man's best friend. Lomax was behaving as if his belly was being scratched or rubbed. Yet in the triangle of shadow next to the cement stairs, he was the only living creature that could be seen.

Leaving Nicholas standing alone behind them, his friends stared in confusion at the animal's inexplicable behavior. They were not concerned at the moment with the girl's picture in the locket. Seeing is believing, as people say, and seeing Lomax not respond was a reason to be inquisitive. Reid was the first to speak. "What's going on?" he asked. "Why is he behaving like that?"

Nicholas looked around to make sure that there were no kids in listening range before he spoke. Staring at the back of all their confused heads, he decided that if timing is of the essence, the time is now.

Nicholas spoke loudly and plainly. "The girl in the locket must have loved animals."

They turned around and almost in unison asked the question, "Why?"

The boy moved forward and knelt down between his friends, facing the large animal. In a patient voice, he simply said, "Come on, boy." The dog responded immediately, leaving the rest of the group speechless.

Afterward, Nicholas allowed the paramedics to examine him to see if he had any injuries. The entire process took about fifteen minutes, and the only medical attention he needed was a small bandage that he applied himself. He walked around to check on the children and staff. They all were fine but were very apprehensive about speaking to Nicholas. They hadn't had an incident of this magnitude for a long time, not since the murder of a young female resident named Monica Lamestra.

The paramedics had a few side conversations with local police officers that Nicholas did not hear. The police didn't have the slightest idea how the office had been destroyed, but they knew that it would need reconstruction. They also said if anyone had been in there during the event, they would need more than just a Band-Aid. There were holes in the walls, and floor tiles were torn up. Summer's metal desk was flipped over and dented, while everything else was either cracked, torn, or smashed. The wallpaper was ripped off in spots, and there were deep scratches in others. Destroying an office like this would probably take five men twenty minutes to accomplish, yet the entire event was over in less than ten minutes, and not a soul was found in the building besides Nicholas, and he'd walked out the front door with hardly a scratch on him.

Detectives Reilly and Arbor stood by Nick's side through all this and protected him from the media and questioning by other police. They, along with Donna and Reid, planned to allow Nicholas to be at The House of Young Hearts on paper but not in person. But before anything could take place, they needed answers. And getting answers to their questions would require a certain level of finesse. What they were about to deal with was uncertain, and the answers were most likely bone-chilling. It was beyond anything that police, military, child psychiatry, or child counseling were equipped to assess. From this point on, they would be Nicholas's protectors, friends, and family. Their concern and sense of responsibility went well beyond what their jobs required. Here was a boy who was homeless and had no family. As great people do, they answered the call, no matter how frightening the circumstance or the outcome.

The group decided that if they were out of sight, they would be out of mind, so they headed to their vehicles. Donna, however, didn't move. She wanted some kind of answer before they left. This threw a bit of monkey wrench into the detectives' plans but was effective. Nicholas walked up to her as the others listened. He looked deep in Donna's teary, confused eyes and said, "The girl in the locket has been visiting me for years, appearing as a shadow on my wall. Today she saved my life when other shadows attempted to kill me. This action indicates that she needs my help, just as I need yours. I'm not insane, but you already know that, and together we can all make a difference."

When Nicholas turned to walk toward the vehicles, Reilly glanced at the picture in the locket Reid was holding and told Nicholas, "I believe you one hundred percent." Reilly then walked up to Nicholas and extended his hand, "Please call me Brian, Nicholas." Detective Arbor, who respected Brian more than any man that he ever met, also extended his hand in friendship and asked Nicholas to call him Zack. Brian then turned to the group. "The first case I ever worked," he said, "was at this very building. The crime was the murder of a young girl named Monica Lamestra. She'd turned eighteen a few weeks prior to her murder. She was suffocated and left behind the building in the open field, barefoot and wearing only a nightgown. The murderer was never caught, and no fingerprints were found and no motive was ever determined."

Brian's story had them in tears. Donna clung to her son, receiving the comfort she needed as she cried. Nicholas noticed that Zack's eyes were welling up with tears, because his eyes were doing the same. Brian, on the other hand, casually acted as if something obstructed his vision and then looked down and walked a few paces in a small pattern, focusing on his shoes.

Reid gave the locket back to Nicholas. Nick then walked over to Summer and asked, "How are you doing?" The woman simply responded with a slight trembling smile and nodded her head to indicate that she was okay. Nicholas then handed her the locket that she had lost.

Summer opened it and stared at the picture of Monica. Summer gently closed it again. "Nicholas, I think you're an amazing young man with a special gift." And with that, she reached out her arm and offered the locket to Nicholas. "Please," she asked, "you keep it." Nicholas accepted the gift and thanked the woman for her generosity.

He caught up with the group and they loaded into their vehicles. Before getting in the back seat where he normally rides, the last passenger wagged his tail, looking back at the building and howling a long good-bye.

Shadow Chapter
NUMBER
Seven...

The three vehicles drove off, heading away from Providence. Brian and Zack led the small convoy, followed by Donna and Nicholas, with Reid riding solo in his own car in the rear. Nicholas did not let on to the paramedics that he had bruised ribs and a severe headache, since he felt that tending to the children's needs was more important. But his injuries now made riding in the truck with Donna rather uncomfortable.

Donna now revealed that she and Reid had a surprise in store for him. They were going to sign him into the orphanage, but then give him the option of living with Reid instead, at least until he was older and able to venture on his own into the world. Summer had agreed to cover for them by putting Nicholas on the books as a resident, as long as he remained in the care of Dr. Anderson. Summer told Reid that if anyone questioned Nicholas's whereabouts, she would inform him immediately. Nicholas told Donna that he was sorry for scaring her and making her cry. He then explained that he'd sworn to himself that dealing with shadows was going to be a problem that he'd tackle without help from anybody else. Donna told Nicholas that they would always be there for him, and then she grinned confidently. Nicholas felt the new circle of friends he'd been accepted into were now like family.

Brian led the team deep into the woods in Connecticut, well past the Rhode Island border. The bumpy road had no street signs that Nicholas could discern. At the end of the secluded road, they came upon Reid's home, a large, custom-built house with a three-car garage and an enormous porch that wrapped around the back of the house. A chimney rose from the stone foundation on one side. Most of the roof was slate, but one section entirely comprised of skylights. The interior used hardwood in some areas and marble in others. The kitchen ceiling, where the skylights were located, was more than twenty feet high. The room given to Nick had its own fireplace and a television set that was monstrous in comparison to any he'd ever seen. As he looked around, he imagined that the house must be hell to clean. He remembered how bad it was cleaning his room at home, and that was only twelve feet by twelve feet, not counting the closet.

At the moment, Nicholas was not too concerned about shadows, but they were a current reality just the same. For now, however, he would settle in and concentrate on dealing with the investigations that were sure to follow after his parents' deaths and the incident at the orphanage. He knew that the police would question him again and that bringing his parents' killers to justice would be a drawn-out affair, filled with trial and error. Nicholas also knew that other child psychiatrists would examine him and cross-examine him, trying to find flaws in his story. Brian and Zack could only shield him from so much. Eventually he would be a piece of meat on somebody's table. It was just a matter of time and a question of when.

During the day, between clients, Reid worked with Nicholas on how to beat psychiatric questions. In the evening, the detectives drilled him relentlessly on how to answer police questions. The detectives decided to prepare Nicholas for the worst. Most of their questions seemed inadequate and off the wall. They pitched questions from all angles, varying their words in attempt to pick up flaws in his story. Brian and Zack stayed at their jobs during the day, acting as if the Johansson case was simply just another case. They never let on, not even to friends or family, that they had a personal involvement.

He spent late evenings blanketed by Lynn. He held permanent trust in her watchful, caring eye. Nicholas had an idea of his own on how Lynn could assist him if he were hypnotized. If she was inside him, she could feed him the answers that the interrogators would want to hear. It sounded good, but Nicholas didn't know how he could get Lynn to speak to him. He can feel what she feels when she's inside, but that was the extent of it. Their communication had been limited up to this point. Maybe, he thought, things would progress at a faster rate now that he's had physical contact with her.

During their questioning, the detectives badgered Nicholas to the point that he almost forgot it was training and not the real thing. Their goal was to break him down on an emotional level. Hearing his voice crack or seeing a glassy eye or a tear was a sign of weakness. The process was designed to ensure that interrogators would not pin the murder of his parents on him. The press would have a field day with a story like that. "A Boy Killer" would probably be the headline. Simply destroying someone's life for the sake of a sensational story of lies is not far-fetched for some newspapers.

Failure is not usually something to be happy about. But Brian, Zack, and Reid were ecstatic when they realized they couldn't break Nicholas. He could have easily earned an academy award for his performances throughout those weeks. His ability to maintain eye contact was amazing, and his competent answers were right on the money. He never appeared overly mortified or cold and heartless. In everything that he said and did, he was a model of concentration.

Nicholas also never called upon Lynn for help. Nicholas was completely alone in the process. He held in his true emotions and used sound judgment instead of feeding off of pain. He made his goals for the future the priority, and this drove him to the success that he needed.

The real police questioning eventually came to an end, but the reporters were reluctant to quit their pursuit to seize a story, even weeks after his parents' funeral. The press followed Nicholas, snooping around the orphanage, taking pictures, and asking questions. They were around so much that he had to modify the living arrangement that Reid and Summer had agreed upon. Pretending that he lived at The House of Young Hearts each day and each night became stressful. He would sneak out through a basement window after lights out, meeting Reid or Brian for transportation. The other kids never ratted Nicholas out when he wasn't around for breakfast the next morning. They were scared of him, to say the least, and this fear kept them quiet. Quiet for how long was the question.

Nicholas was amazed at how selfless his friends were. Their concern for him grew more each day, like adoptive parents with a new child. On the night before Nicholas's parents' funeral, he had an in-depth conversation with Reid, Donna, Brian, and Zack. He started by thanking each of them for their constant contributions to his life. Nick then looked at Dr. Anderson and said, "Outside of my parents, I've never had an adult role model, not until Reid came into my life. My bond with Reid is as tight as any brotherhood could ever be." He then asked the doctor, "What did you mean when you said, 'You have succeeded where I failed. You're winning the battle against the shadows'? Could you please tell your story? It could help me further understand my own."

Donna looked at Reid with a hurt look on her face, as if Reid had deceived her in some way by not speaking to her sooner about his shadows. Reid began his story. "When I was a boy, the shadows made the floorboards creak and moved the curtains while I lay in bed. Many times they would stand next to an open window in the breeze. This would allow the curtains to cover them so that I could see their silhouettes.

"One time, a little after dark, I was walking home from a friend's house, and I felt a presence closing in on me. I didn't see anybody, but I began running home just to be safe. As I ran, I could hear the feet smacking the pavement behind me getting closer with each step. The running footsteps stopped when a hand reached out and pushed me to the ground. I frantically searched around me for a person or an animal, anything to explain how it happened. But there was nothing to be seen. After that, the ghostly activity never took place again."

Reid turned to Donna and explained to her that he loved her with all of his heart. Protecting her was what he felt was best. Nicholas nodded his head in understanding as he listened to Reid's explanation. He could truly sympathize with the desire to protect loved ones, both mentally and physically. At the same time, he could see why Donna's feelings were hurt. Either way, he knew that Reid and Donna would work things out without feeling resentment about past decisions.

Reid and Donna sat side by side on the coach across from Brian and Zack. Before either of them had a chance to speak, Nicholas asked Reid, "Do you know the approximate date that your last shadow experience took place?"

Reid didn't hesitate with the answer. "My last sighting of a shadow was the day you were born. Do you believe in fate?"

"Hey, I'd believe in the tooth fairy," Nicholas said, "if someone said that he or she was real." He immediately apologized for the silly comment. "Sorry. I use humor as a tool to cope when stuff gets out of control." Judging by the looks on his friend's faces, this problem was still too new to laugh about. They understood where he was coming from, but they weren't at that point of comfort yet with this strange topic.

Reid stood up and paced the room for a bit. "Nicholas, I've always had my suspicions that you were dealing with a supernatural force of some kind. My only problem was finding a way to address it or get you to openly discuss it. Neither of those scenarios ever took place, so the conversation never happened. I remember when I first saw your birth date on the case file when it was brought to me. The idea of a comparison between our two situations was a long shot, but at the same time it was always on my mind."

Reilly then spoke. "When I was in my early twenties, I was also attacked by a shadow." Nobody expected the detective to spill out a story like this, but he did. "While I was on a camping trip," he continued, "me and a friend lit a fire and cracked open a few beers." The friend in the story happened to be a girl, so Brian had the undivided attention of four fifths of his audience. "My friend went, shall we say to answer nature's call next to a large tree a few hundred feet from where we were camped. She'd only been gone for a few minutes when I was pinned to the ground by invisible attackers, unable to move my feet or hands. My sleeping bag was being wrapped around my head, cutting off my air supply. As I gasped, it felt like someone was repeatedly punching me in the stomach. Tent stakes were then driven through my pants legs and shirtsleeves. Thankfully, before I blacked out from the lack of air, my female friend arrived and saw what was taking place. She then let out a scream, which alerted other campers, who then quickly came to investigate the call."

Reilly then looked at Nicholas and said, "The answer to Reid's question that you asked earlier is yes! Yes, you do believe in fate," he told the boy, "and if you don't, you should."

"How can you be so sure?"

"Because the attack on my camping trip also took place on the day you were born."

Zack may have had a story of his own, but he didn't tell it that night. Maybe he thought everyone had heard enough, or maybe he felt Nicholas had had enough for one day. Nick was standing near one of the fireplaces in Reid's living room. His back was to the group. A tear rolled down his cheek and eventually dripped off of his chin and splashed on the hardwood floor. Donna stood up, gathering her car keys and coat. She was so confused that the only thing she could do to organize all this shadow insanity was to walk away. As she walked past, Nicholas she noticed the puddle of tears at his feet. Though no one said a word, she stopped herself at the door. Nicholas didn't turn his head, but when he spoke, he asked Donna not to walk out on him now, telling her she was the closest thing on earth that he had to a mother. Donna wasn't going to leave anyway. She put her keys on the table and dropped her coat on the rocking chair in the corner.

Donna rejoined her son back on the couch, holding his hand tightly. The room was very quiet. Donna smiled across the room at Brian and Zack. She took a deep breath, releasing it calmly. "Nicholas," she said, "would you please tell us your story from the beginning?" He wiped away his tears and turned around to face them. "There is no other place," said his mother by fate, "that I would rather be, and no story interests me more than yours."

Reid listened more intently to Nick's story than he had to Brian's story with his chick in the woods. He didn't move a muscle; in fact, he almost had to remind his eyes to blink. Everyone in the room focused on the speaker, but each person felt different emotions as they listened to the story. Reid and Brian could compare it to their own experiences, but Donna and Zack were taking it all in differently. Most people can solve a math equation that involves adding two single digits. But how many can solve an equation in advanced quantum mathematics? All learning starts with a basic starting point, laying a foundation for more advanced understanding. Reid and Brian had a personal, face-to-face understanding of the topic, but as far as Nicholas knew, Zack had no prior shadow experience and Donna definitely had none.

Poor Donna sat listening to Nicholas's tales of daily horror. She didn't know whether to cry or vomit. The kid unraveled years of stories leading up to his most recent attack at the orphanage. His stories were elaborate, detailed, and definitely not bullshit. Each listener in the room had experience sifting through other people's lies and half-truths, and none had any doubts that Nicholas's stories were directly from his heart and soul. They left the room speechless and deeply saddened after Nicholas was done. The teenage boy had spoken for nearly three and a half hours, bringing the group up to speed on what they were up against.

When he had said what he felt that he needed to say, he asked to be excused so he could be well rested for his parents' final farewell the next day. Nicholas kissed Donna on the cheek and bid good night to the men in the room, shaking their hands before getting a glass of water and heading to bed. Nicholas's stories were told with pure conviction, and this earned him the complete respect of his friends. They were proud to know him, and he was proud to have them by his side.

The next morning, Nicholas was nowhere to be found. Reid had asked everyone to stay the night so that they could travel as a unit to the Johanssons' funeral. As the others searched the house unsuccessfully, Brian paused to think. He'd been involved in twelve manhunts during his career, so this small case would be a breeze. Knowing your subject is a key factor when looking for someone, so Brian eliminated the obvious. The boy definitely wasn't in the house, for Brian had heard Nick's name called at least seven to ten times with no response. Brian put himself in the shoes of an upset teenage boy, calling upon his own past experience as a teenage boy. This led him out the back door to the unlocked barn in Reid's yard.

The detective stopped about ten feet from the barn. From behind the half-open door, he heard Nicholas speaking to someone. "I wish you could speak to me," the boy said. "I know your name is not Lynn. It's Monica Lamestra, isn't it?" Reilly stiffened as he heard the back screen door swing shut. The others had followed him after they figured out Nicholas was not in the house. He raised his right fist into the air to caution them. They proceeded carefully down the stairs and across the lawn. Brian signaled for them not to speak as they drew near. He then pointed at his eyes with both fingers and then at the open door leading into the dark barn. The four crept closer in unison—six feet, four feet, two feet—until each of them could see the amazing spectacle.

Nicholas was standing in the middle of the barn. Next to him was an upside-down bucket with a flashlight propped up at a forty-five-degree angle, casting a beam of light on the wall. He was standing to the left of the light, holding the open heart-shaped locket in his left hand. On the dusty barn wall they could see the silhouette of a girl with long straight hair. She appeared to be naked, judging by the contours of her figure. And she appeared to be reaching out, holding Nick's free hand while nodding her head in some kind of agreement. Brian assumed that she was the shadow of Monica Lamestra. Her head nod had to be her way of answering Nicholas's question about her real name. Nicholas took a step closer, cutting into the flashlight beam. As he stepped forward, Monica turned and pointed at the group watching. They all jumped backwards, accidentally bumping the barn door and blowing their cover completely. Nicholas knew that they were watching the entire time, and he was not angry with them for being curious. What concerned him was the fact that they could see what he saw.

Now that the barn door was open all the way, filling the space with sunlight, the beam of light on the wall was almost imperceptible. Nick put the locket around his neck, tucking the heart portion inside his shirt. He reached for the flashlight and clicking its switch to the off position. Brian then asked Nicholas in a low quiet tone if the girl on the wall was the girl in the locket. Nicholas nodded while scratching the back of his head and said yes.

Everyone remained quiet, as if they were holding a telepathic conversation among themselves, trying to decide what to say next. Donna was quiet, because she didn't see anything. Nicholas knew this immediately when he looked at the expression on her face. Donna had a heart of gold. She was not a person who could lie, cheat, steal, or hide emotion. Nick looked at the others. Though he'd never spoken of it, Zack must be able to see shadows, for his face was the same greenish shade as Brian's and Reid's. Maybe Detective Arbor was trying to show strength in front of his mentor.

Nicholas closed the barn door and fastened the rusty latch so it wouldn't blow open. The group piled into Reid's gray Jeep Cherokee parked in the driveway. The drive to the funeral was not as uncomfortable as Nicholas had imagined, even though he wished it were all a bad dream. He was amazed that more time hadn't passed since their death. It seemed that so much had taken place, it left him a bit lost in the shuffle. Several hundred people attended the funeral and the wake. People Nicholas had never seen before paid their respects. Many even spoke of the Johansson family, mentioning their community service and their great ancestry, which reached back hundreds of years to the time of the Vikings.

People expressed their remorse and treated Nicholas with great respect. They commended him for having the ability and stability to move forward after enduring such a huge loss. Not one person looked at Nicholas crossly or let on that they thought he may have been responsible for this disaster. The sentiments expressed made the day easier than he could have ever imagined.

Topping the list of kind visitors was Nick's old buddy, Jimmy Meideros. Jimmy had on a black suit and tie. He was looking good and still sported that winning Jimmy Meideros smile. His family paid their respects, hugging Nicholas in sympathy for his loss. Jim's family walked on, but Jimmy remained behind with Nicholas. Jim attempted to hold his characteristic smile, biting his inside lip while he searched in vain for the right words to say. Nicholas broke the silence. He leaned in close and whispered to Jimmy, asking him if he remembered the night in the sewer, the night when the defenseless, homeless man Oscar Gallo lost his life. Jimmy's smile disappeared. His face became grim as he recalled the night in the sewer, a night that he wished he could forget.

"Is that incident related to your parents' deaths?" Jimmy asked.

Nicholas nodded as he glanced around at all the faces in the crowd. He patted Jimmy on the shoulder and said, "When I know, you'll know." Jim nodded back at Nicholas and then headed over to sit with his parents.

Nicholas knew exactly what was responsible for the death of his parents. But this wasn't the time or place to elaborate on that subject, both out of respect for them and the fact that he was being watched by people in the crowd. Nick wouldn't see Jimmy again for many years to come. He hoped that some day Jimmy would open his heart and mind and confront him about what they saw that night. His tale could unravel the mysteries and would answer many of Jim's questions.

Reid kept a close eye on Nicholas through all of this. During the entire funeral he wondered to himself if Nicholas's strength, both physical and mental, were at all abnormal. He knew that extreme circumstances can heighten human abilities, allowing people to accomplish amazing feats when needed. Strength, speed, agility, and even courage can be enhanced exponentially. But these kinds of events are rare, and the heightened condition normally lasts only a short period of time. It was almost as if Nicholas was designed to withstand what he was currently going through. If that was indeed true, it would mean that fate does exist and can be scientifically proven. Reid wondered how he would have reacted if his parents had been killed after he'd had the opportunity to know them. He would never actually know, of course, since he was orphaned only a few weeks after his birth. But he knew that if his foster mom Donna passed away from illness, accident, or worse, his life would never be the same. Reid chalked it up to the fact that Nick was just a tough kid.

After the funeral, the five of them walked together back to Reid's Jeep without worrying if anyone saw them. Brian, Zack, and Donna climbed into the back seat. Nick rode shotgun next to Reid. Reid looked over at Nick from the driver's seat and saw him gazing at the photo in the heart-shaped locket. It was then that he told the boy he was going to officially adopt him, with the stipulation that he keep the name Johansson for as long as he lives. Nicholas closed the locket and said thank you to the caring doctor. Donna had never been so proud of her accomplished son as she was in this shining moment. She'd truly raised a scholar and a gentleman.

There were many twists and turns on the dirt road in the cemetery where the Johanssons would be laid to rest. Some of the bumps caused Nicholas to whack his cranium on the roof of the Jeep. He ended up with a sore spot, but for some strange reason, the bumps triggered a tremendous idea. He turned around in his seat and asked Reilly, "Why didn't you assume that shadows were responsible for Monica's murder in the first place? The girl was outside, barefoot, in her nightgown, and alone in an empty field prior to her death, wasn't she?"

"Well, an idea like that wouldn't have occurred to me before you and I became acquainted. I see things a lot more clearly now since we met. The only problem is other law enforcement personnel may not be as understanding when it comes to topics of this nature. In fact," the detective went on, "many events in my life seemed unexplainable until now. I was afraid to draw comparisons between my one experience with shadows and work-related events. The idea did come to mind very often, but I always dismissed it as coincidence. It seemed like ignoring the facts was easier than facing the notion that we are not alone, not even when we're by ourselves."

After the burial service, they returned to the house. The adults had coffee while Nicholas had a glass of cold milk and a few cookies. The cookies were store bought and hardly comparable to his mother's homemade ones. While everyone was munching and sipping their drinks, discussing various topics, Reid asked Nicholas a rather off-the-wall question: "Do you believe there's life on other worlds outside of Earth?" The question made all who heard it raise an eyebrow. How, they wondered, was this of any relevance at the current moment?

Nicholas swallowed the milk that he had in his mouth and replied, "Gee, I never really gave it much thought."

"Does my question sound insane?" Reid asked. Donna, Brian, Zack, and Nicholas all hesitantly nodded in agreement. If you ask honest people a question, expect an honest answer. Reid smiled, acknowledging their response, then explained why he asked the question. "I want to get Nicholas to think on a more abstract level than he's ever done before, to think beyond the room we're in, eliminating walls, past experiences, and all knowledge of shadows. Life on other worlds is probably significantly different than life as we know it on Earth. The goals, desires, dreams, and motivations of other beings would be driven by different ambitions. Our ambitions are primarily based on human stimuli or human needs. A creature from another world, on the other hand, may be more or less complex than we are and most likely not human."

Nicholas and the others agreed that his assumptions made perfect sense.

"I put the shadows," Reid continued, "into a category of the unknown. If they are unknown, there's no point looking to our existing knowledge. We are never going to find an answer that explains what they really are. We are spinning our wheels looking for a human explanation of a life form that doesn't play by human rules. Once we are able to establish a pattern of behavior, then perhaps we can understand them in a different way."

Brian spoke up first. "I agree. Reid's idea makes perfect sense. Criminals are caught using similar tactics. Once you're in the particular criminal's mind, you're able to read their next step as if their thoughts were your own."

Zack is usually very quiet, but he spoke up next. "When Nick's ready, he should start teaching us a thing or two about shadows." Zack looked around at everyone for a response of some kind.

Nicholas laughed, smiling a huge, almost crazed grin.

"What's so funny?" Donna asked.

"Well, since I've got a PhD in shadows, let the classes begin." Nicholas requested that for future reference Monica Lamestra be referred to as Lynn. He explained the origin of the name and how she reminded him of a bikini model from a magazine that he had years ago. Her name was also an acronym that he created: loving, yearning, nurturing, and neglected. Those were the terms he'd selected to describe the girl on the wall. Nobody questioned Nick's request to call the shadow Lynn. Without further discussion, they all agreed to honor his decision.

Donna announced that she was going to make a special dinner in honor of Nicholas, but as she stood up to head into the kitchen, Reid politely asked her to sit down for a moment. Reid stood up from his comfortable spot on the couch, faced Nicholas, and thanked him.

Nicholas was caught off guard, so he said, "You're welcome. But what is the thanks for?"

"It's because of Nicholas," Reid explained, "that I now know that shadows killed my parents when I was a baby." Mouths hung open. The group waited expectantly for Reid to explain his dramatic statement. After Reid once again gave his condolences to Nicholas for the loss of his family. "Through helping you, I may have diagnosed the death of my own parents. They were pushed to their deaths from the balcony of an empty hotel room, behind locked doors. Cameras monitoring the hallway outside revealed nothing. Both of them had severe bruises on their arms, necks, and backs, including many broken bones resulting from the five-story fall. The room itself revealed no struggle or forced entry, and their luggage was never unpacked or rummaged through. I was apparently found after my parents' bodies were discovered. The report said that I was still in my baby seat and crying uncontrollably." Reid went on to thank Donna for raising him and Brian and Zack for giving him access to the file.

Detective Reilly quietly told Reid that maybe someday police reports will provide a section for investigation into paranormal behavior. This way they might be able to lay to rest crimes where there was no human criminal to blame. Reid agreed and said that having a complete array of facts would provide a logical if seemingly insane answer to the unexplainable.

Reid then made an announcement. "Nicholas," he said, "your destiny is to unite an entire world of darkness with the land of the living."

Nick smiled at his friends. "Anything is possible with you by my side." He then excused himself and headed down the hall to take a nap before dinner.

Donna again stood up and headed into the kitchen. As she walked away, the three men in the living room watched in amazement as her shadow followed her into the next room. They looked at the shadow and then at each other. At that very moment, each of them had something to say, but no one said a word.

Shadow Chapter
NUMBER
Eight...

As he lay in bed waiting for Donna's special dinner, Nick daydreamed. Every creature in the galaxy, from microscopic particles squirming in a laboratory Petri dish to a giant eighty-foot sea squid, faces obstacles during their existence. Microscopic life, he thought, had to deal with the possibility that their existence might go unnoticed forever. If scientists never created microscopes, then germs would have remained their own secret society of tiny, invisible killers. Antidotes would be nonexistent, so the population of Earth as we know it would long ago have been consigned to pine boxes covered in dirt. How do I know, he wondered, that a microscopic organism has the ability to worry? I really have no idea. I'm only stating a fact from a strictly one-sided, human standpoint, my own. It's safe to say that if germs were lonely at one point in time, they're not lonely anymore. Their fifty-million-year infectious spree is now a fifty-trillion-dollar industry. What about that eighty-foot sea squid? A giant sea squid is the largest, scariest creature on the planet. Everyone and everything is scared of a monster of that size. They couldn't possibly have any obstacles! Getting enough nutrition to fulfill their daily needs must be a big concern. Being called a mystical monster from the depths of hell for countless centuries must also suck! Where can you hide when you're eighty feet long? Once again, from my strictly human standpoint, he thought, these two completely different life forms share one very significant obstacle, one that is detrimental to their existence, and one that is very resourceful: the human being.

Humans normally retaliate first and understand later. Imagine if you went to dump the trash, and instead of a raccoon you saw a ten-foot tall, thousand-pound Bigfoot waiting to greet you? How would you respond? Would you attempt friendly contact? Maybe say hello, or invite him in for a cup of coffee? As a human, though Nicholas, I'd probably scream like a little girl and run back to my house to look for a weapon. I'm not a violent guy, and I love animals, but in a case like this, instinct determines our reaction.

I'll bet that if, as a species, we took the time to react mentally before physically, many of our dilemmas, situations, and obstacles wouldn't seem so overwhelming. Taking the time to assess problems is also an excellent way to develop as a leader. Other people will see you turn big problems into small, easy-to-handle tasks. If you do this often enough, Nick thought, people will eventually regard you as a level-headed thinker. Using logic rather than rage to get answers and work through problems is the key to success. And in the absence of knowledge, a good leader also has to know when to follow.

Nicholas mind now wandered back to his own problems. He wanted to learn more about Lynn. He decided to follow Reid's advice and try to see the situation through both shadow eyes and human eyes, since he did have access to both. The shadow of a murdered girl and possibly millions of others were counting on him. Who was he to let them down?

It was hard for Nicholas to comprehend that human souls might not exist, that despite how we live our lives, there is no guarantee that the after death will be quiet and peaceful. The man in the sewer believed that to be true. He did not come out and say it, but his final words did seem to contradict the majority of religious systems, which preach eternal rest.

Nicholas squeezed Lynn's heart-shaped locket in his left hand. He wished that he could rub it like a magic lamp and summon her to appear like a genie, but her appearances were sporadic. His eyes were closed tight, but his heart and mind were working overtime. At one point in history, microscopic life was unnoticed and large sea creatures were considered monsters. But now both of these life-forms are regarded as living organisms of this world we call Earth. In time, he thought, the shadows would eventually become a phenomenon known worldwide, beings with their own category, somewhere between science and religion. Nicholas's mind went back to when he was eight years old and saw his first shadow outside the living room window. His memories of that night were full of fear and anger. He had retaliated, but with the intention of protecting his loved ones, not out of concern for himself or hatred of the unknown. Once a theory of shadows is proved, he thought, the masses will accept it.

Nicholas lay down to rest, having exhausted himself in complicated thought. His grip on the heart-shaped locket loosened. Lynn then connected with him as she did in the orphanage during the battle. They became one. This time her smell radiated through his pores. Her skin was softer than before, and if Nicholas rubbed his fingers together, he could feel the texture of it like it was his own. This new experience was different from their first meeting in the closet. It was more of a sensual rather than sexual connection. Without a doubt, Nicholas thought, they were perfectly matched partners. Before, Nicholas only saw with his eyes, but now he could see on an advanced level that others rarely conceived.

Nicholas was lying down when he heard a woman's voice calling to him. "Can you hear me?"

He sat up in the bed and replied, "Donna, is that you calling me?" He waited. "Donna, is that you?" But there was no response. And when he looked in the hallway, it was empty. His room was also empty. As he sat there on the edge of the bed, he realized that the voice had come from within. Nicholas looked around the room and then whispered under his breath, "Lynn, are you trying to communicate with me?" He was so nervous that he didn't move a muscle until she responded.

"Yes, Nicholas, I can speak from within you through our thoughts. There is no need for a voice. Spoken words," Lynn went on to explain, "are intended to pass from mortal to mortal, not mortal to shadow. Shadows can only talk to the living once they are inside a Compatible. A Compatible is a person like you who accepts a connection from a shadow like me."

Through force of habit, Nicholas started to speak in words again, but he quickly stopped himself. He then thought of questions to ask Lynn. Thinking of what to ask her first was the hardest thing, so he went with an easy question to start off. "How long have you been attempting contact? If you could have spoken mentally sooner, why didn't you?"

Lynn said, "A compatible connection isn't an instantaneous bond like a relationship that two humans would develop. As shadows, we have to share experiences on a level that is measured by responses from the human we try to connect with. I wanted the timing to be perfect for you, so I waited."

Nicholas sat on the edge of the bed with his back to the door, feeling confused and a bit sad. "I assumed fate had something to do with us connecting." Nicholas closed his eyes and asked, "How did I get the impression that what we have is a magical, almost perfect bond?"

"Our bond," Lynn said, "is more than a one-hundred-percent connection. You and I were made for each other in every way except in the relation to time. Connections are not bound by time, as far as I know," she said. "Shadows are already dead, so they can't age. A person could have died five hundred years ago then suddenly meet a compatible in the year 3000. Time has nothing to do with a connection. Only the connection itself matters."

Nicholas then asked her to tell him more about the shadows that kill, as opposed to the ones like her. "Rippers," she began, "are demons from the shadows. They can appear like good shadows in order to make contact. They target easily manipulated humans or evil and greedy humans. In the end, they end up dead. A Ripper can leave a person as easily as a Faith Finder like myself can. The only difference is that when they leave, they take your life with them. Had death not brought me to the shadows and given me the ability to find a Compatible," she said, "our lives would never have crossed."

"Did you ever pass through my body before the attack at The House of Young Hearts?"

"I've been there since the night you impaled your arm on the knife as a boy. If I hadn't stepped in that evening, the shadow outside the window would have."

"What would have happened?"

"You would have been killed instantly, due to your condition and age. Shadows like myself only connect for life and love." Nicholas was quiet again for a while, and then he asked for her to explain more. "Shadows," Lynn said, "cannot contact other shadows or see them unless they are trying to contact the living. When contact of any kind happens, we can all see it from the shadows, as long as it is in direct sight. Direct sight, however, is not obstructed by walls or barriers. After death, shadows have no memory of time or events. All that remains is a need to be found and accepted. Shadows remember nothing from their human life except how they died. Our death stays with us as a reminder that we are lost and forgotten. I can now remember small things from my life because we are connected and you are alive. This link allows me to communicate and feel. And in an abstract sense, it gives me a second chance at life within you, Nicholas, my Compatible."

"Do you know about the murder of my parents? That was shadow to human contact of some kind."

Lynn apologized for his loss and told him that it was not in direct view, so she was unable to see it.

"How about Oscar Gallo, the homeless man killed in the sewer? Why didn't you try and prevent that from taking place?"

"I can only go inside people that allow me to, otherwise I'm powerless to help someone. Nicholas, are you optimistic or pessimistic?"

"I feel that I'm an optimist," he replied.

"Open-minded people see things in a different light. A pessimistic person is very self-involved, engrossed with their own problems. They wouldn't help an injured person or animal if it was right in front of their face. People like that only notice what directly involves them. Some people are so negative, they selectively see and hear only what they want to, with no regard for anyone else. A narrow-minded person sees a shadow as a flutter of light on the wall. You, being an optimistic person, see a life rather than just a shadow."

"If there isn't contact between shadows, how do you know the terms Rippers and Faith Finders?"

"Humans eat, sleep, and breathe, don't they? Shadows search and connect, or search and kill. Once we are dead in the shadows, all we know is our own title and the title of our opposites."

"Do you remember exactly how you died?"

"I died of suffocation. One man watched me die. The man who ordered the shadows to kill me had a special power over them that allowed total control. I was a very quiet girl who'd lived at The House of Young Hearts for the majority of my life," she told Nicholas. "All of my dreams and goals were taken from me when Conrad Buggleport introduced himself. Buggleport was an old man with wild gray hair and thick glasses. He wore normal clothing, a sweater and dress pants. When he stepped out into the fog from behind the fence that concealed him, he wore a grin of pure evil. I knew from that moment that this might be the day I was going to die. I'd never met Conrad Buggleport before that evening. I was barefoot, wearing only my nightgown. I think the shadows were the ghosts of my deceased parents trying to make contact with me. Buggleport watched as I attempted to run away. He never tried to stop me himself. He only laughed, muffling his enjoyment with his hand. The shadows did his work for him. They quickly grabbed me, strangling away my young life for the pleasure of a fiendish old man."

"Why would shadows work for a mortal man? Wouldn't they rather kill him themselves?" he asked.

"I don't know," she said. "I'm a Faith Finder, and I can only be controlled by a Compatible of my choice. A Ripper may need something more. What that is, I don't know. I only know the needs of my own kind."

As Nicholas sat there on the bed, he believed more than ever that he was a chosen hero set on a path to stop a madman. Now all he had to do was find him.

Nick's shadow girl changed the topic of conversation by complimenting him on the lovely pet name that he'd chosen for her. Nicholas could sense that she was changing the topic to avoid any more questions. He, on the other hand, had so many unanswered questions that there was no alternative but to keep asking, despite her wishes. His next question brought an aggravated tone to Lynn's voice. "Do you think our contact together could have prompted the Rippers to notice us and thus created the opportunity to attack my parents?"

Her answer was bleak but detailed. And it was a nearly perfect substitute for an answer she either knew or didn't want to lie about. She described her world outside of Nick's body. "Before we connected, my existence was filled with gray clouds that filled endless, black, angled corridors. It appeared that there was a floor, but my feet could never touch it. The ceiling and walls had geometrically shaped openings that led to other corridors, also absent of sound and light. In the shadows, not all humans can be seen, and only some can be heard. A combination of the two is rare, and the potential for connection is more limited than that. Your parents may have had their own involvement with the shadows that you don't know about. Perhaps the Rippers can see in the way that Faith Finders do, and your parents unfortunately became a target. Either way, I am truly sorry for you, Nicholas, but this is all I have for now. You and I will learn more as time goes on, but for now we need to learn more about the gift we have together.

"You are a man of honor and respect. You proved this during the attack at the orphanage when you stood up and challenged the Rippers alone. You are also kind and respectful to others, both living and shadow. Your strong sense of conviction, loyalty, and self-respect will guide you to the truths you seek. The only flaw I can see is that you are impatient, but this will improve with age and experience. Joining two worlds is not an easy task, but I'll be by your side through it all."

Nicholas stopped communicating for a moment and waited to see if Lynn was going to elaborate on her last statement. She spoke about connecting two worlds. This was an idea that Nicholas hadn't shared with her yet, since they only began mentally chatting with each other not more than a half an hour ago, so he straight up asked her, "How long have you been reading my mind? And why can't I read yours now that you have human thoughts inside of me?"

"I already explained," Lynn said, "that I've been passing through you since your accident at the age of eight."

This response still did not answer what he'd asked, and his patience with their telepathic conversation was starting to wear thin. Lynn giggled at Nicholas's temper tantrum. "What the hell do you think is so funny?"

"We're having their first argument, and it's because I told you the truth and you can't handle it." Nicholas laughed, but he laughed out loud instead of telepathically like Lynn. They both apologized to each other and continued their conversation.

Nicholas could now see where Lynn was coming from when she said that he needed to work on his patience. His mother was the last woman to have given him the same advice. He asked Lynn if she knew how long it would be until he had the ability to read her thoughts. Once again, she did not have an answer for him, but she did say that she was a virgin at this experience too. That made Nicholas happy, and he could sense that she was sincere when she said this connection was her first.

"If we had established contact earlier, it might have permanently destroyed the bond that we share now. At eight years old, a voice in your head from a shadow on the wall would no doubt hinder the developmental process. I was also apprehensive to speak to you, because there was a chance we might not be able to bond. So I waited patiently in the shadows, watching you as much as I could."

"If you had me in direct view, why didn't you watch me all the time?"

"That's a good question, and deserves a good answer, but all I could see is what I could see, nothing more. At times, the shadow world is sightless and soundless, opening its curtains to your world only here and there. These are things I remember but cannot explain." Nicholas thanked Lynn for all the years of protection and for answering all his questions. "If you didn't ask any questions of an older woman living in your head, that would be strange." Nicholas smiled and unclasped the locket so he could see her pretty face as she spoke to him. "I can also see through your eyes. My focus is your focus. Seeing myself alive in the small picture from the locket makes me sad."

Nicholas stood up from his spot on the edge of the bed and stretched until his back cracked. He started slowly pacing around the room, scratching his head as he tried to think of more questions. At one point, he stopped and leaned against the bureau, with his palms facing the mirror and elbows extended by his sides. He released a long sigh and stared into the reflection in front of him. While staring in the mirror, he also looked behind him for any Rippers that may be watching, waiting for him to be alone. Nicholas asked Lynn if she was still there, at first out loud and then through thought. Knowing when to use one or the other is easy, but it's confusing when you're tired. She responded, telling him that he looked very tired, to say the least. Maybe she was reading his mind, maybe she wasn't. Either way, however, the statement couldn't be closer to the truth.

"Lynn, I have one final question to ask you before Donna, hopefully, calls me to dinner."

"You go first, but I have one question for you too."

"Is our connection going to be temporary or permanent?"

Lynn did not answer immediately. She said, "I can answer that without saying a word."

"How?"

95

"Look directly into the mirror and it will reveal the answer you're searching for." She then showed her last living form to him through his own eyes.

Nicholas was a teenage boy approaching the age of sixteen. In his short time on earth, he'd experienced many feelings, some traumatic, others astounding, but most unexplainable until now. Although Nicholas was very mature for his age, both physically and mentally, physical and mental strength alone aren't enough to fool Mother Nature. He was still going through puberty, and his body was undergoing uncontrollable chemical changes. A quick-witted woman could easily push the buttons of persuasion in the mind of a man at this stage. In some cases, these imaginary buttons become harder to push as a man matures, although it still can happen, despite a man's good intentions.

Lynn was able to slip through the loopholes in Nicholas's questions. Her response to his question about whether their connection was temporary or permanent was answered in such a way that Nicholas could draw his own conclusions if he wanted. Being forced to draw your own conclusions can be misleading but at the same time satisfying, but the answer you end up with, like beauty, is totally in the eye of the beholder.

Lynn revealed herself to Nicholas in her last form, beautiful and untouched. Her long black hair flowed freely to her waist, shimmering with a silky radiance. The rest of her was perfect, equal to a sculpture created by the hands of an artist. She was incredible as she pranced on a stage that was set for only Nicholas's eyes to see. While he watched her through the vision she granted him, he couldn't help but feel sad that such an incredible creature was dead. Nicholas couldn't imagine how someone could have been so evil, ending this innocent girl's life for some sick gratification. He closed his eyes as he leaned against the bureau. While he stood there, he thanked Lynn for what she showed him. Her vision slowly faded from his view as Donna entered the room to inform Nicholas that dinner was ready.

The boy looked up at her and replied, "I'm right behind ya." Donna left the room. After talking to Nicholas, she had a strange feeling that she'd interrupted something, but she was scared to ask what. Before Nicholas headed down the hall to join the group for dinner, he opened the black, heart-shaped locket to see Lynn's smiling face one more time. He then closed the locket, simultaneously shutting off the light to the room. As he headed down the hall, he had Lynn in his heart and Conrad Buggleport carved into his mind.

Shadow Chapter
NUMBER
Nine...

Good things can happen to good people, but good things can also happen to bad people too. When this occurs, people remember loved ones who lived well but unfortunately died before their time. Each us at some point in our lives will lose someone close, either by illness, accident, murder, suicide, or old age. The expression "dying before your time" shows that people weigh loss in terms of how an individual was appreciated when they were alive here on earth.

When a man wakes up after a long coma, people usually marvel at it as a medical miracle. And medical miracles are normally looked upon as events to rejoice about. Not so in the case of Conrad Buggleport. His resurrection brought nothing but disgust to the people who knew him. His very existence was a curse. He was a condoning host to viruses that Nick Johansson knew all too well as Rippers. What Nicholas doesn't know is that when he eventually discovers Buggleport's awakening, it will be a key factor in exposing the shadows. If Buggleport was once a gateway for Rippers, he may once again serve the same purpose.

In the meantime, Nicholas enjoyed his life and his conversations with Lynn. The two of them discussed all sorts of scenarios involving shadows and humans, covering all possible angles and leaving no stones unturned. They agreed on many of the possibilities when they were backed by hard evidence that justified them. Things that they didn't agree on weren't forgotten. Instead, they gave those topics special attention until they came to an agreement. Time was not an issue that Nicholas and Lynn worried about. As long as they had each other, it seemed that time stood still, so counting the clock wasn't necessary. What was necessary, however, was to follow the rules.

Nick and Lynn wrote five rules to govern what they learned, how they learned it, and what to use it for. These rules were also put into place for protection.

Rule One:Humans and shadows should never unite unless
     the bond can benefit both of them.
Rule Two:Benefiting from a connection can never be for
     evil or financial profit; a bond of that
     nature is only for Rippers.
Rule Three:Rippers may appear friendly for a connection,
     but the connection will lead to the death
     of the human involved.
Rule Four:Life with a shadow is not a guaranteed
     partnership; after death, time will always
     be undetermined.

Rule Five:Keeping secrets is a fatal mistake that can lead
to insanity when joined by a shadow;
honesty is the only reality.

Once the rules were set in place, Nicholas and Lynn planned to
go out into the world looking for others like themselves. They
wanted to teach people to understand the difference between Faith
Finders and Rippers. If more people had an understanding of what
they were dealing with, shadows and humans could coexist. Like a
cure for a disease, this information would be the beginning of the end
for the Rippers, and their ability to kill the scared and weak would
diminish.

As their game plan materialized, all of their hard work seemed to
be paying off. The only problem was that Nicholas wasn't comfortable
with how Lynn answered some of his questions. On many occasions
he felt that her answers veered in a direction that was truthful but
vague. He felt that maybe he should word his questions differently or
more directly. Her evasive answer to his question concerning their
eternal bond was one that stuck out in his mind. Nicholas thought
back to the night he asked the question and the wordless explanation
that he received. Lynn's answer really was not an answer at all. Nicholas
wanted to know if their connection would benefit the two of them
equally. He was also curious to know whether their connection, if
permanent, would become a necessity for future survival. Nicholas
was fine with the possibility of living life with Lynn. His main
concern was to know whether the bond was equally beneficial to
both, in accordance with the rules they'd agreed upon.

With Lynn's constant assistance, the painful burden of puberty
was easy to bear. She was never short of energy or burdened with the
problems of a human girlfriend. Lynn never had to wear makeup or
spend large amounts of cash to be happy. Their relationship was
simple, if a complex situation can be explained that way.

Another slight problem that Nicholas faced was not knowing just
what Lynn could or could not feel or read while inside his body.
Thoughts that were directed toward her she could hear, but she
never commented on his normal, everyday thoughts. This was not
currently a problem, but over time it could quickly become one.
Lynn knew that the deaths of his parents and the man in the sewer,
Oscar Gallo, and the story of her own death weighed heavily on his
mind. Obviously these things would concern him, but Lynn knew the
exact moments when they concerned him. And this raised a red

flag in Nick's mind, leading him to think that his assumption about Lynn reading all his thoughts was possibly correct.

One day Lynn asked Nicholas if he ever considered the notion that his parents brought the shadows on themselves by accident. Nicholas was so irritated by her question that he asked her if she was trying to piss him off. He told her that she had mentioned that a while back, and the answer was no then and it was no now. Lynn took Nicholas's response as a form of mistrust. She had never seen him react like that to her before, even though she had her suspicions. She sometimes reads his thoughts, but she never mentions this to Nicholas or how often she is able to do it. Both of them were dealing with trust issues that neither of them chose to admit.

Nicholas's uncertainties varied as the weeks and months passed. Every thought he had was not his alone; it was actually theirs. But her thoughts were hers alone and impossible for him to hear. All Nicholas sensed was an inner expansion and contraction that felt like intestinal gas, but it was obviously Lynn reacting to his thoughts. His newest concern was whether she linked up with him for her own reasons and not to create a perfect bond. When Lynn was a shadow, Nicholas thought, she already said that she searched for a Compatible without human reason involved. Her bond with him would have had to be purely for survival. She said herself that back then she could not think in human terms. Nicholas now doesn't know if she's a liar or a Ripper in disguise, waiting for a chance to strike.

Lynn felt these thoughts of confusion raging inside Nicholas's brain, polluting his body and breaking his heart. Her first reaction was to separate herself from him completely. Yet this would mean she might possibly be lost forever in the realm of the shadows. The rules they created together were tested to the best of their ability. They were like two castaways on an island who were forced to make the best of it. After she considered her life without him and the alternative in the shadows, Lynn decided to give it time and hope for the best. Nicholas was a young man in an odd relationship. Though simple to comprehend, this fact was difficult for Lynn to accept. Lynn understood that the human brain was very complicated. Thoughts are constantly forming, often contradicting one another, in a giant spool of overanalyzed data. Lynn took the pain of Nick's thought pattern personally; it was hard for her to ignore, and even more so because she was in love with him.

How many females have the ability to literally read their man's every thought? If women possessed this ability, men would be in big trouble on a daily basis. In the mortal world, men and woman would never even have the chance to meet, never mind date. Passing each other on the street would lead to heated arguments if the woman heard the thoughts behind the man's friendly hellos and smug grins. The only positive aspect of female mind reading is that there would be fewer broken hearts for the girls and fewer divorces.

On the other hand, the ability would have negative consequences, drastically altering the world. If dating disappeared, for example, the restaurant industry, vacation locations, credit card companies, movies theaters, and flower shops would lose billions of dollars, because far fewer people would be visiting these establishments or using these services. And men's approach to meeting the opposite sex would have to change, since their not-so-well-thought-out one-liners would be useless. Their time-honored, hit-or-miss strategies would be useless against a woman who knew their ultimate goals. If the shoe was on the other foot and men could read women's minds, men might be slightly repelled, but they could probably live with the gift. When two people first see each other, attraction is initially a physical thing. Their thoughts can be perverted or romantic or a combination of the two. Either way, however, internal thoughts belong to the originator. As long as we keep some of them to ourselves, we are entitled to that luxury.

Lynn stuck to that same rationalization of thought as a helpful tool to stay on course, despite her hurt feelings. As time went on, she seldom questioned Nicholas's thoughts, and they matured together. Their discussions were leading into more complicated issues, combining science with the supernatural. Lynn nurtured the hope that Nicholas would gain more patience. And he wished that she appreciated the patience that he already had.

Reid and Brian had an idea that bordered on being a stroke of pure genius. They felt that for Nicholas to reach his goal of contacting people with similar shadow-related experiences, he would need to broadcast his message on the radio. This approach would protect his identity and would be effective in getting his point across to a large audience. The two men brought their idea to Nicholas one Sunday afternoon while he was carving a sculpture out of a block of wood on the back porch of Reid's house. Brian sat down next to Nicholas, and Reid leaned against the railing a few feet away from the pile of wood chips Nicholas was creating. Their timing couldn't have been better, since Donna had recently arrived and Zack was on his way. Nick was only in early stages of creation, but it was looking like a sculpture of a man and a woman.

As Donna walked up the path, Nicholas stood. He greeted her with a big smile and a hug. Donna said hello to the guys and asked Nicholas what he was making. He said it was going to be a statue of his mom and dad holding hands. They were all supportive of his current project, and Brian told Nicholas that it was coming along well. Reid then asked Nicholas if he was interested in hearing about another potential project. He assumed that since Nicholas was in the midst of flexing his creative muscle, this would be a great time to present their idea for a radio show.

Reid and Brian laid out the plan. They both had their share of contacts, so getting to the right people to start the project wasn't a problem. For practically pennies, they could have a show on an AM station three nights a week, on Sunday, Monday, and Tuesday. The only problem is that it would air from eleven fifty until ten after midnight. Those hours aren't exactly prime time, but if someone is sleep deprived due to shadow involvement, there's a chance that they may be listening and looking for help.

Donna didn't want to let on how she truly felt about all this shadow talk. She was concerned that her son and Detective Reilly were getting in too deep. At first she thought that they were supporting Nicholas as mentors, but now she wasn't so sure. A rumble from the driveway turned everyone's head. It was Zack pulling up on his vintage '67 Indian. Zack removed his helmet as he walked up the driveway. Brian commented that it was a perfect day to take the bike out. Zack agreed. He tapped fists with Nicholas and said hello to the others.

The group resumed their discussion about the radio show and brought Zack up to speed on their endeavor. Lynn waited inside to see Nicholas's response. Part of her thought it was a fantastic idea, but another had worries. Her concern was Rippers. If a Ripper was inside of an evil person and they heard the show, Nicholas would be a target for attack. Even though his identity was safe, they would eventually find the location of the station and possibly where he lives. Lynn could protect Nicholas against Ripper attacks from shadows alone, but she was powerless to protect him from an assault by a Ripper inside of a human. This concern of hers was something that they needed to discuss in private. She knew that if she explained this potential problem to Nicholas, he would definitely understand. Bringing an attack on his friends would be horrible, and it would mentally ruin Nicholas if they were injured. Their idea for the show came straight from the heart as supportive friends. It's too bad they had no idea what a Ripper was capable of, especially one inside of a mortal.

Nicholas asked if he could think the idea over and give his response in the morning. That statement from Nicholas to his friends proved to Lynn that her opinion did matter. She felt an acceptance from him; it was something that she needed to hear as a woman. If she had separated from Nicholas when her thoughts were based on pure emotion, she would have been a hypocrite. How could she point the finger at Nicholas for acting impatiently, when that's exactly what she was about to do?

That evening the two of them lay in bed, mentally discussing the positive and negative aspects of the radio show. Nicholas listened to Lynn's pros and cons, and she did the same for him. At the end their discussion, the matter was still basically unresolved, for they had difficulty in making a precise decision. Either way, there were risks and rewards.

Morning arrived. Nicholas opened his eyes immediately. He noticed a large cone-shaped beam of light cutting through the open blinds, creating a cylinder of light across the room where he slept. For a moment he thought that he was back in the hospital and looking at the light from the window that Lynn danced in. Then he remembered that Lynn no longer dances on walls. She is a part of him now, and if she wants to dance, they can dance together. All of a sudden, another thought from his stay in the hospital crossed his mind. He remembered that he tried to avoid falling asleep that night but still fell asleep anyway. He recalled peeking one last time at the room and seeing that there was another shadow standing next to Lynn. The shadow was as large as the one that appeared in his living room window on the night of his accident. Nicholas quickly asked Lynn if she remembered watching him fall asleep in the hospital room that night.

"I have no memory of what took place when I was a mere shadow," she replied. "I've explained that many times before, but you inconveniently never listen."

"If you have no memory of shadow life," he asked, "how do you know that you protected me from attacks?" This question was drawn from something Lynn told Nicholas on a previous occasion.

During her short life on earth, Lynn had been a very smart girl compared to her peers. She had an IQ of nearly 160, with scores in science and math equivalent to a person holding a master's degree in engineering. Lynn responded to Nick's question. "I don't know. I'm sorry. It was wrong for me to dismiss the possibility that as a shadow I had no memory. I thought that then, but now I believe something different." In closing she offered another apology.

Her answer to the question would have sounded sincere to someone who wasn't looking to sift through bullshit, but Nicholas was in the mood to sift. "Do you care to tell me anything else, since we're on the subject of what you could and couldn't remember?"

"What, exactly, are you referring to?" Lynn asked.

Nicholas said, "I want a truthful answer. Who was standing next to you while I was falling asleep in the hospital room eight years ago?"

She could hear the frustration in his voice. "Will you agree not to be angry at my response?"

Nicholas agreed. "I won't be angry as long as I don't get mad."

Lynn didn't know how to respond to that comment, so to be on the safe side, she made her answer short and sweet. "I don't know," she said to the cranky teenage boy. "I don't remember that night. Maybe in the future I'll know more, but now that's all I know."

Nicholas did not get mad. He thanked her for her answer and then completely changed the subject. Lynn was caught off guard by this, but at the same time she wasn't surprised, since Nicholas's questions were sometimes random and unexpected. The next topic of discussion was whether to accept or decline the radio show. After their lengthy discussion the previous night and the continuation of it this morning, they agreed to disagree on the answer of yes. There was a high risk that Nicholas would be attacked by Rippers joined with evil mortals. Nick and Lynn's entire mission revolved around reaching out to others like themselves. Anything involving such a mission could be fatal; whether or not they pursued the show, this they both knew and understood. Whichever way the coin fell, they would stick by each other's side as one unit.

Nicholas jumped out of bed and got dressed. He didn't realize that it was six thirty in the morning when he walked into the empty living room. Suddenly Reid walked up behind him on his left side and tapped him on his right shoulder. Nicholas turned to his right, startled by the tap. Reid smiled. "Want some breakfast?"

"Sure."

"So, what's the verdict concerning the radio show?"

Nick sat at one of the stools at the counter and said, "I'd be interested in starting immediately."

"Your answer is music to my ears, because I have the keys to the studio and the contract ready to go." Reid opened one of the drawers in the kitchen and slid the stuff to Nicholas. "Why don't we both eat and then head over to the studio to check it out."

"You must be reading my mind," replied Nicholas.

Reid raised his eyebrows and said, "Maybe I am." The man's response was a harmless joke, but since Nicholas knew Reid didn't cast a shadow, anything was possible. Thoughts of mind reading left Nicholas's brain almost as quickly as they entered, although the boy was still a bit creeped out.

During the ride to the studio, Nicholas and Lynn mentally discussed the kind of reaction that they wanted from their listeners. Nick was holding two conversations at once, one with Lynn and the other with Reid. Lynn said that since she can't speak out loud for others to hear, she wants him to speak of her presence on the radio. Nick suggested that her name on the air should be something exotic. Lynn said that her stage name will be The Shadow Princess. Nicholas smiled as he looked out the passenger window. He told her that his will be The Viking.

The studio was not at all what Nicholas or Lynn had imagined. The outside of the building looked condemned, as if it was ready for a wrecking ball or a bulldozer to knock it down. The interior was clean but looked very old, like Summer's office back at the orphanage. Regardless, they were both very thankful for the opportunity. Reid, Brian, Zack, and Donna assisted Nicholas that evening in cleaning up his new studio. It's amazing how much of an improvement can be made to something with some good old-fashioned elbow grease and lots of cleaning chemicals. By the end of the day, Nicholas and Lynn had a desk, a chair, and a freshly painted studio free of mouse droppings. They were all ready for business on their first night, which happened to be that coming Sunday.

The big night finally arrived, and Nicholas was sitting in the hot seat waiting for his first call. The Viking had planned to accept all calls, both foolish and serious. Some people called to ask The Viking questions, and others called to ask The Shadow Princess questions. Occasionally a listener called in to yell and scream or say something derogatory just to hear their voice on the air. On other nights, nobody called. That's life on the open air.

As the weeks went by, some of the same callers would call back, either to talk or engage in a short conversation. Because the shows were only twenty minutes long, Nicholas had to limit each caller's time. On one particular evening, a shy young lady called in. With a very monotone voice, she asked, "Have I reached *The Shadow Inside* program?" After Nicholas said yes, she asked, "Is your show meant to entertain people or to help them?"

The Viking approached her question by first complimenting her on naming the program. "Thanks for suggesting such a cool name for our program. I hadn't named the show yet. Your title, however, fits perfectly. And thank you for asking a serious question rather than hanging up or blurting out an obscenity."

She then introduced herself in a slightly more upbeat sounding voice. "My name is Eleanor Strude," she said. "I would like to know if the topics you discuss on your show are ever exaggerated."

Since he hadn't had a chance to answer the lady's first question, he attempted to knock it all out in one breath. "I wish to help people. Nothing I discuss is ever exaggerated. If anything, I may sugarcoat certain topics rather than relive my own pain with each explanation. I want my listeners to reach out to me because they are in similar circumstances, not out of pity for me."

"I've been listening to your show ever since the first night it came on the radio," Eleanor said. "I saw a flyer hanging on a pole in Providence informing the public of when to tune in. Are you aware," the lady on the line then asked, "that they perform crimes, cause accidents, and in some cases kill?"

Nick looked around the small studio, biting his lip and fiddling with his audio equipment while he thought of a way to respond. He did not want to sound too eager or anxious in answering Eleanor's strange question. At the same time, he wanted to jump on the desk in front of him and scream into the microphone like one of his nutcase callers. If this woman could ask such a definitive question, Nicholas thought, she must be connected to the shadows. This lady was reaching out for help and most likely knew true fear on a level most people can't even fathom. He replied to her with a long question, long enough to get a trace on her phone number. Detective Reilly had not only helped organize, clean, and paint the studio, he'd also hooked Nicholas up with police equipment to track phone numbers. The gear Nick was using was pretty high tech for the eighties, considering it was probably from the seventies. But it served its purpose, just like the studio they were using. Brian's original idea was to be able to track area codes through the calls. This way Nicholas could establish a pattern of where the most frequent calls originated. Each show was also taped so that Nicholas could review his monologue and note changes he wanted to make for future broadcasts.

He asked Eleanor, "Do you actually know a person who was victim of a shadow attack or accident?" The woman didn't respond, so Nicholas reworded his question. "Do you feel comfortable mentioning the victim's name on the air?"

Her voice resumed its original monotone, for she felt boxed in by his demand for an immediate answer. She shot back with a question for Nicholas. "Will my response be more beneficial to you or the listeners?"

Lynn was listening inside Nicholas the entire time. When Eleanor thrust the questioning back to him, Lynn giggled. To both their surprise, the joke was on them, because Eleanor had somehow heard Lynn's giggle. "Are you sitting with a female co-host?" she asked.

"No," Nick responded, "why would you ask such a question?"

"I heard a woman laugh." She paused and then said, "The laugh must be from the dead girl inside you, Nicholas Johansson." And with that, her monotone voice turned into a cackling, evil-sounding laughter that filled the studio. The laughter was so hysterical that Nicholas yanked his headphones off and pushed his swivel chair back almost five feet from the console. Before Nicholas could speak, Lynn demanded that the woman tell her if she was joined with a Ripper or a Faith Finder.

Eleanor Strude laughed again and said, "Conrad Buggleport says hello."

The air remained silent from both sides as the clock ticked closer to the end of the show. With exactly thirty seconds of air time remaining, the voice on the line asked, "Nicholas, are you still there?"

"Yes," he responded.

"Viking was a cute choice of name, but your parents would have liked Nicholas better."

Nicholas stood up out of his chair and shoved it clear across the room, smashing it on the far cement wall. Breathing heavily, he roared at the laughing witch. "Explain what you know of my parents!"

But Eleanor said no more. Only static filled the room. The show was over, but more incoming calls were lighting the board up like a teenager's face pocked with acne. Before Nicholas unplugged the entire apparatus from the wall, he noticed the number on the caller id box. It had a 317 area code attached to it.

"The woman called from Indiana," Lynn said to Nicholas.

Nicholas snapped at her. "How the hell do you know that information?"

Lynn didn't appreciate Nick's tone. She simply replied, "I read it from the mind of the Ripper inside Eleanor. And anyway, the fact is, the caller had a phone number starting with area code 317 and Rhode Island's area code is 401. So even if it wasn't Indiana, it was obviously another state." Lynn's remark was snide and sharp. After her explanation, she led into the woman's comment about the flyers on the telephone poles. "How did she see our flyers on the telephone poles? They were only visible for a few hours. Not after the three days of rain we had. Last, but not least, our program was on an AM station, so what are the odds that Eleanor Strude could even hear us in Indiana?"

Lynn's points were valid yet irritating, considering how aggravated the boy was. Nicholas didn't need any more irritation, since he was already past his boiling point. He grabbed his bangs with both hands and stared at the ceiling, trying to refrain from ill-conceived words or actions. The frustrated adolescent sat on the floor and let out a deep breath. "How could you feel through a radio wave to a shadow eight hundred miles away?"

She made the mistake of asking Nicholas to be patient while she explained. Just then, Reid and Brian quickly came through the door. Nicholas stood up feeling tired, irritable, confused, and stressed out. He apologized for smashing the chair and offered to pay for it. Nicholas was a troubled young man who needed and deserved real answers to his questions, especially after his last caller's comments. Brian observed the signs of this and glanced at Reid. Through each other's eye contact they both agreed that Nicholas had enough for one day.

Donna entered a moment later, noticing the smashed chair in the corner of the room. She had listened to the show and heard the horrible things that the woman on the line said to Nicholas concerning his folks. On top of that, the woman commented about Nicholas's shadow friend, and that scared the hell out of Donna. Donna agreed from the beginning to stick by Nicholas no matter what, and that was what she was going to do as a social worker, a mom, and a friend.

After this incident, the radio show did not air again, nor did Nicholas ever attempt to contact more believers. He now believed that his answers were not to be found through informing the masses about shadows. His answers and the heart of the problem lay in Indiana, where the killer of his shadow woman may still dwell.

Shadow Chapter
NUMBER
Ten...

Between the time that Nick and Lynn's radio show *The Shadow Inside* ended and his eighteenth birthday, they were able to work out most of their problems. Many other things took place during those few months, including saying farewell to his good friend Detective Brian Reilly.

Brian was not only one of the top detectives in Rhode Island, he was also a sergeant first class in the National Guard. Brian had been a loyal service member for nearly nineteen years and had served his nation in many conflicts. Brian now was offered the opportunity to be a master sergeant in a Special Forces unit based in Hawaii. This would be a promotion and a great opportunity to lead some of the best Green Berets in the United States Army. He knew that if he accepted this position he would have to relocate away from his full-time job, friends, and family. Nineteen years ago, Brian took his oath as a soldier and then later as a noncommissioned officer. Even at the beginning, he was aware of and prepared for the commitment ahead, no matter where the journey would take him or how dangerous it might be. The Providence Police Department and the Rhode Island Army National Guard held ceremonies commemorating Brian's selfless service to the shield and flag.

Prior to Brian's departure, Reid also threw a big going-away party at his house. The party was enjoyable but very sad, to say the least. During the party, Brian and Nicholas had a moment for guy talk to express what was on each of their minds. Nick was upset over losing a friend, but Brian cleared up that misconception for him very quickly with two simple statements. "Some friendships," he explained, "are everlasting, and no distance can ever break a bond that doesn't want to be broken. If something is worth fighting for, then it's worth dying for, but that decision has to be made by the man fighting the battle and nobody else." Brian spoke with such conviction and pride that Nicholas understood why his friend had to leave for his new duty assignment.

Some people are made to live basic lives, and others live exemplary lives that give basic people goals to strive for. The man who stood before him had substance, substance that derived from a place in the heart which most people never see. To rob a man like this of his ambition would be a sin. All you can do is wish him well and hope he'll return to complete the loop of a successful, lifelong friendship.

Brian Reilly said his good-byes and respectfully declined the many offers to drive him to the airport the following morning. Nicholas assumed that even a hard man needs time to himself, time to be with his thoughts and reflect on his life. The detective-soldier made a very positive impression on Nicholas. He would be missed very much but never forgotten. Nicholas felt that the feeling was mutual, so that made his pain tolerable. Watching Brian say good-bye to his life in Rhode Island fueled Nicholas's ambition to keep fighting through the unknown to tackle his own uncertain future.

As far as the law was concerned, Nicholas was now a man. He had crossed the magical line of eighteen years and was now legal for some things but not others. Nick had a small inheritance that his parents had left for him, along with some cash that he earned as a bar-back at Conley's Bar in Warwick, Rhode Island. The owner of the bar was a big burly Irish fellow named Patrick Conley. Patrick didn't really care too much that Nicholas was only eighteen, as long as he didn't drink any booze on or near the property. The bar got pretty rough on some nights, and Patrick was glad that he had someone else around who could handle himself if the situation called for it. From almost any angle and in almost any light, Nicholas appeared to be no younger than twenty-five. A conversation with him would only reinforce that assumption.

In addition to his job as a bar-back, Nick also bused tables and, if needed, worked the door, checking IDs. On some weekends, he had to ask rowdy belligerent customers to leave. On other nights, he was forced to give them the grand tour of the gravel parking lot by any means necessary. Nick also broke up fights, which were mostly fights between girls at Conley's Bar. Nick was often the victim of a wild sucker punch or a well-directed kick to the family jewels.

Patrick Conley was a very generous guy. He tipped Nicholas well for his hard work, leaving his pockets full at the end of the night. During his entire shift, Nicholas hardly said a word, not unless spoken to. He was driven to save up ten thousand dollars toward the purchase a 1970 Buick Riviera. Nicholas wanted black tinted windows, high performance suspension, and Cragar chrome wheels. To complete the package, the car also had to have a 455 GS Stage 1 engine.

Nick suggested to Lynn that they should consider relocating to Indiana in the future. In Indiana, he could work days as a farm hand and spend his evenings hunting Conrad Buggleport and his army of evil Rippers.

Lynn kept Nicholas's mind occupied at work. Even a focused man would be occasionally thrown off balance by what he saw at the bar on any given weekend. Women hit on Nicholas. Though they seemed to know he had a girlfriend, they shot him many unnecessary smiles and attempted other forms of distraction. He would politely tell the girls that he was in love with someone else and that this special person was also his best friend. Then, with absolute sincerity, Nicholas would thank the lady or ladies for their flattering inquiry. Yet despite his honest efforts, not all of them got the message. Some people want what they can't have, and they become persistent, even pushy.

Persistence comes in all shapes and sizes, and a dose of it mixed with persuasiveness can be lethal, if administered correctly. One evening, Nicholas was unloading a large beer delivery behind the building. The truck arrived at the bar on time that day, but was stuck there due to engine problems. This actually was a blessing in disguise for Nicholas because the bar was understaffed that day. He'd been carrying kegs and boxes for about a half hour when a gorgeous blond and brunette approached him from the shadows. Nicholas started in on his well-rehearsed and very polite, please-go-away speech. But these girls didn't want to discuss anything. They wanted immediate action.

Completely disregarding Nicholas's plea to be left alone, the blonde stepped in, rubbing her hand down his chest while the brunette undid his belt buckle. Nicholas stepped backwards and tripped on the truck ramp behind him. He dropped the keg. The metallic smash echoed in Nicholas's ear as he lay on his back. One of the girls started laughing, while the other asked if he was okay.

As Nicholas stood up and brushed himself off, he felt Lynn's tears running down the inside of his cheeks and down his face. She could sense that Nicholas wanted the women who approached him. Lynn was aware, of course, that Nicholas was a human being. But she felt heartbroken, nevertheless. Her feelings were so powerful that they actually registered in Nicholas's facial expression in full view for the women to see. The blond stopped laughing and rudely asked Nicholas if he was retarded or something. The brunette reached toward his face to console him, asking why he appeared as if he was going to cry.

Patrick had heard the loud bang from the bar's kitchen. "What the hell happened?" he asked when he came outside. Nicholas didn't respond. He just turned around and picked up the freshly dented keg that he'd dropped. Both of the girls quickly walked away. They too ignored Patrick's question. Patrick walked up to Nicholas and said, "Look, son, you're by far the best employee I've ever had work for me. Nobody comes in early and stays late without complaining, but you've never complained, not even once. And I usually have to remind you to take your paycheck with you when you leave. If you've got a problem, feel free to discuss it with me." After staring him squarely in the face,

Patrick patted Nick on the shoulder and started toward the building. As he walked away, he had one last thing to say to Nicholas. "You know, Nick, talking about stuff isn't a sign of weakness. Shadows can't solve your problems."

Nicholas gently put the keg back on the ground and took a few steps toward Patrick. "Hey, can you repeat what you just said?"

The man turned around, surprised to see Nicholas walking up behind him. He then repeated his statement. "I've seen you mumbling to yourself here and there as you worked. It looked to me like you were talking to your shadow, that's all."

Nicholas stared silently at the man, who was almost at eye level with him. But Lynn told him to walk away and forget about it. She said that all he was doing was making an observation. He's neither a Faith Finder nor a Ripper. Looking down, Nicholas saw the man's shadow cast by the light of the moon, and he concurred with Lynn's observation.

Patrick stayed put and watched Nicholas head back toward the truck. The man shook his head. "Nick, why don't you take a break. Come on in and grab a burger and Coke. I'll finish unloading the truck as a little thank-you to my best employee."

Nick didn't look up or argue, he simply entered the back door of Conley's Bar and went into the kitchen area. Big Conley did as he said he would and started unloading the truck. All the while, however, he was puzzled. Why would a statement about mumbling and shadows set Nicholas off? Inside the bar, Nick took his burger and coke to a secluded back booth, away from the noise, crowds, and cliques that hung there. He was absent-mindedly selecting random french fries, dragging them though a river of ketchup, salt, and vinegar before eating them. He chomped on his dead cow dinner but discarded the remainder of the bun. Lynn finally spoke up and told Nicholas that patience goes both ways, and that she was not mad at him at all. Nicholas slurped his soda while resting his forehead on his left hand. He unclasped the black, heart-shaped locket and took a gander at Lynn's picture. Suddenly, however, a familiar voice asked if the seat across from him was taken. Nicholas snapped the locket shut and hid it under the table as he looked up at the visitor. The man who owned the voice was Detective Arbor.

"Say, isn't your name Zack or something like that?"

Zack laughed. "If you keep that up, you'll be calling me detective instead."

Nicholas smiled and offered the seat across from him to his old friend. "So, am I under arrest for underage burger eating at a bar?"

"No, no jail time just yet," Zack said sarcastically. "But does Dr. Anderson know you work here?"

"Catering jobs and fast-food joints don't pay any real cash," he explained to the young detective. "I love the doc like an older brother, and it's time I start paying the man back for all he's done." Nicholas explained the stipulations that Patrick Conley set forth as regulations governing his employment at the bar. "Please, Zack, don't bust the man for hooking me up with steady work."

Zack nodded in agreement. The sweaty Swedish giant then slid his leftover fries over to the detective to seal the deal. Zack refused, saying he was trying to maintain a healthy diet, free of excessive carbohydrates and unwanted saturated fats. His statement sounded way too rehearsed to Nicholas, too canned to be a hard-core belief, even if it was backed by the best intentions. Nick slowly crunched another fry heavily caked in salt. All the while, he was grinning a sarcastic smile, doubting that the detective was all that faithful to his carb-cutting rule. Arbor took the hint and reached for a fry.

As he stretched across the table, a red-headed woman wearing a half shirt and tight jeans walked by, smiling in Zack's direction. He was so blindsided by her obvious interest that he accidentally bumped Nick's soda, sending the poor basket of french fries tumbling toward the filthy floor. Nicholas simultaneously grabbed the soda and caught the basket of fries, narrowly avoiding a messy catastrophe. Zack regained his senses and apologized for his clumsiness.

"You ought to indulge yourself more," Nicholas suggested. "The ladies seem to like you. In the long run, you'll develop a steadier hand, saving the life of more barroom food."

Zack smiled and then inspected Nicholas's attire. He was wearing a T-shirt that said "I'm a very bad boy" in boldface print. He wore a studded bracelet on his right wrist. It appeared that he had a self-made tattoo that said "STAND ALONE" over a scar on his left forearm. His bangs hung to his chin, almost totally blocking his eyes, though Nicholas could see fine. On his left wrist was the black rubber band, possibly serving a purpose that Zack didn't ask about. Zack swallowed his french fry, then he asked Nicholas, "Did you get a chance to read the remainder of the Buggleport file that Brian left for you?"

"I read every single word, but I was confused. Why did Brian leave it on my bed instead of handing it to me directly?"

"Brian really admires you," Zack said, "and he felt that you would want to find out the news on Buggleport yourself."

Nicholas looked at the detective with a very confused look on his face. "What news are you referring to?"

"Was there a newspaper article somewhere in the file?"

Nicholas waited for the follow-up to the detective's statement, but there was none.

Finally, Zack continued. "The article reports that Conrad Buggleport awoke from a coma after all these years."

Lynn uttered a distressed no in response to the horrible news the detective was telling them. Judging by the level of fear in her voice, anyone would think that the man was standing right in front of them at that very moment.

Nicholas couldn't believe it. He leaned across the table and asked Zack, "Are you absolutely positive?"

"Everything is in the article. Go home and read it for yourself."

Nicholas then asked a question that he should have asked a long time ago. "Okay, but tell me one thing. Did Brian really work the Monica Lamestra case?"

"Why are you asking questions that you already know the answers to?"

Nicholas ignored his question. "They never found a fingerprint or determined a motive in her case. All they found was the body, isn't that correct?"

Zack nodded his head. "What's your point?"

"If there was never a suspect, where did the name Conrad Buggleport come from? Can you explain that, detective?" Nicholas asked rather abruptly.

Detective Arbor did not respond right away. He sat back in his seat and looked at Nicholas with a puzzled glare. By the sound of it, he seemed to agree with Nicholas's assessment and to share the boy's confusion over this new revelation pertaining to the case. "Hmm. I have access to all the same records that you already read. When the murder actually took place, I was still in junior high school, so I followed the information that was given to me by the police department when I became a cop. Everyone else in the department said that the case was eventually closed due to insufficient evidence. Yet despite the closing of the case, Brian Reilly on occasion spoke of Conrad Buggleport. I assumed the man was someone who might have heard something, someone who might be able to shine some light on the case. I never thought the man was a suspect."

Nicholas then considered a different course of questioning for the detective who sat before him. Every statement the man gave seemed sincere, and he seemed to reply to the best of his knowledge. Yet there still may have been other elements that hadn't been discovered, elements hidden inside each of the people involved in Nick's life and with the case itself. New discoveries were made all the time that proved supposed facts to be false and falsehoods to be facts. One fact that Nicholas knew to be true was that Reid, Brian, and Zack did not cast shadows of their own. This bit of information could possibly be a huge turning point in the case as well as in Nicholas and Lynn's life together.

The problem was, how do you address an issue like that in a public place without starting an argument or worse. Nicholas couldn't think of what to ask, so he questioned Zack's loyalty toward Brian Reilly as a friend and a superior. He thought that through selective questioning, Zack might inadvertently expose crucial information. He might not learn why the guy doesn't cast a shadow like normal folks do, but he might obtain other pertinent information, information that could later prove vital. So Nicholas went ahead and asked his question.

"Detective Brian Reilly," Zack replied, "was the officer that trained me, right from the time I became a rookie, straight from the academy. Without Reilly's mentoring, I probably wouldn't be as far along in my career as I am."

Nicholas did not need any further verification concerning the depth of Arbor's loyalty. But he decided to probe deeper anyway.

Before Nicholas could ask another question, however, Zack told him that question time was over. "What's the third degree for? I want to know, and I want to know now. Be a man instead of acting like a scared little boy. If you have a question, ask it. Don't hesitate to speak your mind around me or anybody else."

Nicholas stood up and looked down at Zack. "I don't know the first thing about being scared." Nick attempted to walk away.

Detective Arbor snapped his fingers. "Sit your ass down." The cop then slammed his wallet on the table, creating a loud clanging sound with his badge. "First of all, I'm an officer of the law and I deserve a little more respect than that. Secondly, I hate to repeat myself. So sit down and ask me your question face to face like a man."

Nicholas reluctantly slid back into the booth. Every nosey drunk in the bar was looking over at them, waiting to see some kind of show. But the show was over, and now it was time for business. For a moment, the two sat there staring at each other. Anticipating another comment,

Nicholas decided to speak first. Zack looked as if he was preparing to call him less than a man, or a little boy, or make some other provoking, degrading remark. Nick was pretty sure that another insult would lead him to tear the table clear out of the floor. Out of respect for the owner of the establishment, he thought that he better start talking now.

"Okay, officer, here it is," Nicholas replied. "I see shadows, but you already know that. They see me, they harass me, they attack me, and I have one living inside me. Her name is Monica Lamestra, the murdered girl from the case file Reilly left on my bed. I chose to call her Lynn, and she finds the name cute, so Lynn it is. My question is about you, Reid Anderson, and Brian Reilly. Why don't you guys cast shadows?" Nicholas finished his ranting by saying, "There, all my cards are on the table now, so let's see yours, detective."

The detective looked as calm and cool as a man on a hammock swinging away a Sunday afternoon and relaxing with a cold beer. He calmly removed his glasses and wiped the lenses on the tail of his blue polo shirt. Then, after clearing his throat and holstering his wallet into his back jeans pocket, he clasped his hands together on the table in front of him. "We do have shadows seen by mortals, but they can't be seen by people like you, who have a shadow inside. We are a much simpler form of Compatible, due to the fact that we have Dormants and not Faith Finders or Rippers."

Nicholas then mentally asked Lynn if she was aware of this. "I knew of their Dormants," she said, "but communicating with them is rare, so I never mentioned it." Lynn did explain, once again, what they are. "Dormants are depressed shadows who cling to humans for warmth and the feeling of life. Other than that, they are not really good or evil; they're just an attachment, seen and understood by only a few. Their bond is not an agreed-upon connection. They connect where and when they can." This explained why she hardly spoke of them.

Nicholas asked Zack, "Can you communicate with your Dormant shadow?"

"Yes," the detective said. "Conversation may last for a few sentences one day, and then there might be silence for years. The only similarity between Dormants, Faith Finders, and Rippers is that their thoughts spill over into your thoughts." Nicholas asked him to explain. But as the detective talked, Nicholas wasn't really listening. He started to answer his own question, realizing that naming the shadows wasn't really his idea. Lynn had been passing through his body for years, so her thoughts could have overlapped his, leaving the information behind for him to remember. Nicholas tuned back in to Zack. "I can't communicate with Lynn, but Dormants do have another power that I forgot to mention. Dormants have the ability to see all that happens in the shadow world. They are lost, and they are depressed because, unlike Faith Finders and Rippers, they can see more than what is directly in sight. It seems as if that would be a gift, but when you are forced to see all the horror around you, it's actually a curse."

Nicholas interrupted the detective. "Conrad Buggleport's name was given to us by Dormants that witnessed the attack."

Zack's face lit up when the pieces fell into the puzzle together. What the kid was saying made sense. The two men were on the same sheet of music now. Nicholas was so happy to be figuring out answers, that he couldn't bother with being mad at Lynn for keeping their Dormant shadows a secret. The enthusiasm they shared wouldn't last forever, so Nicholas politely excused himself and headed back to work. Before he left, he thanked Zack for his patience and assured him that his mentor would be proud of the great officer he had become.

Nicholas kind of dragged his feet as he headed across the bar's dance floor on his way back to work. In the background, an old love song was playing on the radio. The song was "Unchained Melody." The tune reminded him of that movie *Back to the Future* for some reason. As he listened and walked, he imagined dancing to this song with Lynn in his arms, her long black hair smelling good and her curves captivating the audience as her dress flowed with every sway. He realized how important music was for remembering key moments in life, like a symbolic bookmark placed on the pages that we turn.

When Nicholas was within a few feet of the door to the back room, he looked behind him in the direction of the booth where Zack had been sitting. To his surprise, the man was gone and the table was clean and dry. On this particular shift, the other bar-back on duty was a Mexican kid named Fernando De la Rosa. Nick knew that the kid worked fast, but nobody is that fast. All of the dishes and trash had to have been removed in a matter of seconds. On top of that, the kid wasn't even in the area when Nicholas had begun to walk away from the table, so that made the scene seem even weirder. It appeared as if the table had never been used, even though Nicholas still had a few fries in his left hand to prove it.

The confused Viking stood there with his back almost against the door, staring toward the booth. Inside, his body felt empty, almost as if Lynn had temporarily separated herself from him. If that were the case, all the Rippers in the area would have definitely attacked him by now. This would have been their chance to initiate yet another violent surge. Nicholas remembered how Lynn had been concerned about him getting involved with the radio show. She thought that Rippers who were inside of evil Compatibles would surely find him. He felt that her concern was both appropriate and admirable, befitting a caring woman in a relationship. Despite the hardships they both faced, he knew her place was with him.

The old love song came to an end, as all songs do. A couple walked over to the table where Zack had been sitting, breaking Nicholas's concentrated stare as they sat down. He looked away. As he reached into the ice machine for a handful of frozen chips, he was approached by three men. All of them had wild smirks on their faces, indicating that the trouble he was dreading had finally arrived. Lynn broke her silence. She warned Nicholas that this was a Ripper attack and that she was powerless to protect him. The man in the middle knew both Nicholas's name and Lynn's real name, Monica Lamestra. He told Nicholas he was a trouble-making punk who knew too much. The Viking could feel the power of his ancestry engaging in his fury as they moved toward him. He did not hesitate to react.

Nicholas reached in fast, grabbing the right wrist of the man to his extreme left. He yanked his arm, pulling him in front of the middle man. As the man on the right attempted to smash a beer bottle over Nick's head, he blocked it with his forearm. He then threw a snapping sideways kick directly to his face, sending him crashing to the floor. The middle man did not react in time. His buddy's head acted like a battering ram, smashing his nose and splattering blood all over his face. All three men were down but not out. The man in the middle was still able to stand, even with the blood streaming down his face. He appeared to be the leader of the three. His hair was red, and his build was rugged and strong. This time he assumed in a fighting stance, indicating that he wasn't that easy to beat. Before his next move, he asked Nicholas how the policemen and shrinks were that manipulate his life. He was just beginning to comment about Lynn when the back door violently swung open.

There in the doorway was Patrick Conley, the owner of the bar. Patrick had a leg to an old table in his right hand and a meat cleaver in his left. He was ready for action and ready to back his number- one employee. Patrick knew that if Nicholas had to clean house this drastically, he must have a good reason. The large Irishman kindly suggested that the red-headed man pick up his unconscious friends and leave. As the only attacker left standing looked at the pair of armed giants before him, he left. Loyalty was apparently not his strong point, because he left his friends there and walked out alone. Once the man was gone, Nicholas and Patrick dragged the other men outside and left them next to the dumpster.

Nick walked quickly to the truck and up the ramp to finish unloading it, as if nothing happened. His heart was beating like a machine gun under orders to expend all ammo. Lynn pleaded with him to sit down and rest. He was dripping in sweat and slightly dizzy from tossing the three men around like pillows. Patrick followed Nicholas at a slight distance. He watched as the boy did the last of the unloading like a team of ten men set to a clock. Patrick grabbed a couple of plastic crates and placed them next to the ramp that was connected to the broken down truck. Nicholas ignored Patrick, while he sat there. He stayed focused trying to get the job done.

This went on for a solid fifteen minutes, until Nicholas stopped working from exhaustion. He'd hoped the owner would just walk away, but it didn't quite work out the way he wanted it to.

Nicholas looked at Patrick and asked, "Do you want to speak with me, or can it wait until I'm done?" The boy stood at the top of the ramp waiting for the man's answer.

Patrick stared back and said, "I meant every word when I said that you are the best employee I've ever had." He stood up from the crate he was sitting on to meet Nicholas as he walked down the ramp. Once at the bottom, Nicholas extended his hand for Patrick to shake, hoping to avoid the spiel about having to fire him. Nicholas thought it must be hard on the man to like an employee as much as he did, but still have to let him go. At least this way, they could both walk away with their dignity intact. Nicholas imagined that it wasn't very good for customers to see him mumbling to himself or beating people up here and there. This alternative worked out best for everyone. Before walking away, Nicholas thanked Patrick for keeping him on as long as he did.

Patrick wasn't about to let Nicholas leave that easily. "Son, a long time ago someone took a chance on me, and things did not go as planned. But the opportunity itself opened up a wide variety of options that I wouldn't have had otherwise." Patrick then handed him a white envelope. Written on the envelope in bold black letters were the words YOUR FINAL PAYCHECK. "Hopefully," Patrick said, "the contents will make your journey more successful, if you use it wisely." With that, the man walked away and went in his bar through the back door.

Nicholas waited until his old boss was behind the closed door and completely out of sight. His mother had instilled good manners in him, especially when it came to receiving a gift in the form of currency. He slit open the envelope, revealing the contents. He was shocked. It was filled with crisp one-hundred-dollar bills. Nicholas wanted to go give it back, claiming that Patrick must have made a mistake, but for some reason he didn't. He then felt a warm feeling of hope flow throughout his body. "For an outsider with the world on his shoulders," Lynn said, "there seem to be a lot of people on your team, Mr. Johansson." He laughed out loud and shook his head in agreement.

The cool night air sent a chill up his spine. The perspiration-soaked T-shirt clinging to his skin made him shiver. He felt good at the moment, enjoying the beautiful night sky. His heart was full of hopeful thoughts as he felt Lynn's smile radiate from within, as it had many times before. Her love and devotion may have come from a shadow, but it felt like a ray of sunshine, even in the middle of the night. The two began their walk home.

Shadow Chapter
NUMBER
Eleven...

Nicholas and Lynn's departure from Conley's Bar began as a happy, romantic stroll. Their conversation and thoughts flowed freely, just as it had when they were initially introduced to telepathic conversation nearly two years prior. Back then, Lynn's ability to read Nicholas's thoughts was not very well developed, but now she not only can read his mind, she has mastered the full potential of her own female intuition as a woman of shadow. This sounds like bad news for Nicholas, but it isn't. All that it means is that her senses are more keenly aware of how he's feeling and how to deal with it. His own uninterrupted thoughts can range more widely, without her questioning every negative vibe. Nicholas has also undergone some of his own changes. He has acquired the ability to blanket his thoughts so that they are only read by Lynn in moments when he is deeply saddened or angered.

They both saw that their relationship was growing in a positive direction. A magical feeling had come over them, somehow allowing their connection to reach new heights. In life, change can happen spontaneously, without a single hint beforehand. These alterations were a silent gift that allowed the couple room to breathe. Perhaps it was a result of the patience that Lynn preached and Nicholas practiced. Or possibly they were both realizing that their hard work toward their relationship was worth the struggle.

The two of them would have fewer arguments as they continued to learn about their bond. A completely perfect bond is a work in progress. They'd been their own worst enemies in the beginning when they created the five rules for the coexistence of shadows and humans. Realizing that the extra pressure of the rules was not needed, Nicholas now had to prove it to Lynn, since he'd been so adamant about following them before.

Every relationship has its share of dead ends, wrong turns, and detours. It's how you maneuver around these obstacles that matters. In the bar earlier that night, it seemed like Detective Arbor simply disappeared into thin air once Nicholas left the table. When Nicholas questioned Lynn about his observation, she replied that she remembered only what had happened after the attackers arrived. The rest of the night was a blur. Nicholas found her answer absurd, since she sees what he sees. But he decided to exercise patience and sound judgment. If Lynn could not remember their dinner break with the detective, then she couldn't possibly remember the two lovely ladies who propositioned him. It seemed like an even trade not to go down that road again, so he kept quiet.

She wasn't completely out of the woods yet. Nicholas wanted to know if she ever had steady conversations with the Dormant shadows or any of the Rippers inside the attackers. The mood of their comfortable evening stroll was about to change. Happy and romantic were about to switch places with aggravating and mistrustful. Lynn told Nicholas that if she thought the information she acquired from other shadows concerned him, she would have said something. Her answer was completely uncalled for. The boy, who was calm a moment ago now, felt disregarded and frustrated. His current mood was clouding his mind like a brewing storm.

As Nicholas turned the corner onto Claritan Street, a few miles from the bar, he noticed an old rusty trash can lying beside the road. Nicholas turned to it and suddenly stomped his size sixteen shoe through the can, making a hole as big as a watermelon. His shoe was completely engulfed in the hole he'd created. Also sitting on the side of the road were an old recliner and a broken mop handle left in a green bucket. Nicholas grabbed the mob handle and stabbed the chair. Then he picked up the recliner, flinging it into the street like a maniac. A few porch lights went on to investigate the noise and commotion. Out in the street stood a giant Viking amid a collection of their destroyed trash. None of the neighborhood people said a word; they just stared at the scene with looks of confusion on their faces. Nicholas addressed their concern by throwing his arms up in the air, as if to ask what the hell they were looking at. The tips of his fingers reached almost to the nine-foot mark, if you take into consideration that he had on combat boots. He then yelled at the top of his lungs, telling everyone to close their doors and blinds and go back to their beds before the chair went through one of their windows. It wasn't in Nicholas's nature to threaten innocent people. The statement sounded better in his head than when he actually spoke it aloud.

He was actually alarmed by his insane action, so he decided to retreat into the night. Retreat is not a word in Nicholas's vocabulary, but in this case he was running away from himself, so that was okay. The boy quickened his pace. He ran so fast that he lost track of what direction he was heading in. The pounding of his combat boots smacking against the pavement actually drowned out the chirping of the crickets that are normally heard around town. Nicholas ran down the street so hard and for so long that he eventually collapsed from sheer exhaustion. He fell head over heels into a puddle when he tripped on a tree branch that was lying on the road in the darkness. The sudden crash brought Nicholas to his senses. He began to think clearly again as he felt the puddle soak through his pants. Between heavily winded breaths, Nicholas began speaking to Lynn. "From now on," he said, "disregard the rules. The five rules were written to add order to our lives. But we need to focus on survival and sanity, not rules." Lynn agreed, no questions asked.

Nicholas sat up, removing himself from the puddle. As he stood up, he could feel the scrapes and cuts from his fall. He slid his sweaty hands through his bangs, which were also saturated in sweat. "I'm so stressed out, Lynn," Nicholas said to the girl inside him, "but I'm never going to quit on us. I will continue this fight until the end. I'm not mad at you for not remembering our conversation at the table with Zack." Nicholas began to walk again. She did not reply, so he continued talking. "And I'm also not mad that you hid information from me that you received from either the Rippers or the Dormants. What I am concerned about is that for some reason I may be losing my memory, and I feel that you are too."

"What do you feel that you've forgotten?" Lynn asked.

"I can't remember who gave me the locket with your picture in it. I also can't remember the faces of the kids at the orphanage or how I got the scar on my left forearm. I feel like these things were just recently forgotten. The strange part is, my memory loss is not in any particular order. I remember my parents, friends, and some events, but not others, even though they may have happened later." Nicholas pulled his bandana out of his back pocket and tied his hair back. He picked up his pace again. He happened to notice some other trash on the side of the road minding its own business. Lynn giggled, as she sometimes does, and asked him if he was going to assault those trash cans too. He and Lynn shared a laugh together.

Laughing is positive, but these two lived on one big emotional rollercoaster. "Observing other couples at the bar," said Lynn, "gave me a chance to think about stuff. From what I saw, many of them have their own problems, maybe even some are similar to ours. If we dissected their lives as we do our own, they may even be worse by comparison. It depends on how you look at it." She paused a few moments and then said, "Nick, there is one fact I can share with you about last night in the bar, if you care to know. The man with the red hair was Conrad Buggleport's son."

"Did the Ripper inside the man tell you that?" Nicholas asked.

"Besides the red hair," Lynn said, "he looks like a younger version of the evil bastard that watched me die. Do you remember the last caller's voice from the radio show?"

"That is something I could never forget, even if I had amnesia."

"Eleanor Strude must live inside of Buggleport's son. I'm not sure, but I have a hunch."

"We should pick up the pace a bit," Nicholas suggested, "before someone calls the cops on us or we get attacked by Rippers. We'll be safe at Reid Anderson's house for the time being."

"Who is Reid Anderson?"

This alone proved that she was losing her memory almost as quickly as he was. Nicholas ran again, heading toward Reid's house. He could feel the effects of the fall on his aching back.

Suddenly a set of high beams appeared out of the darkness like a lighthouse cutting a path of vision for a ship lost at sea. They were located near the end of the road where the houses were scarce and the woods began. Nicholas was going to ignore them, but he felt compelled to walk forward in that direction. As he drew closer to the vehicle, he squinted his eyes to adjust to the contrast of their piercing glow. He moved in on an angle, so that in case the vehicle lunged forward in an attempt to run them over, he could shield himself behind the telephone poles or look for cover among the sporadically placed trees. Nicholas was not armed with any weapons, but having Lynn inside would protect him from an external Ripper attack. His adrenalin was pumping and his fear sensors were waging war on his nerves. He waited patiently in anticipation for the vehicle to move or for the driver's door to open, revealing who or what was controlling it.

From where Nicholas was standing, he could see that the car was the one he had dreamt about. Every specification seemed to be exact. The dimly lit streetlight hanging above them exposed the Cragar chrome wheels, showing off their style. At a glance, the car appeared to be in mint condition. Nicholas remembered a model his father had given to him as a showpiece to place on the shelf in his bedroom. His dad used to tell him that if he thought about it enough, someday he might own one just like it. He was now close enough to see his own reflection in the black tinted glass. In Nick's imagination, he believed the car was driven by the devil himself. He thought that if he was going to hell, he might as well enjoy the last ride he was ever going to have.

The driver's side window lowered a bit, releasing a plume of smoke like a stack on a locomotive. The headlights snapped off. They went dead at the very moment Nicholas noticed the V-shaped hood ornament. This symbol could represent many things to many people, but in this case Nicholas felt that it stood for Viking. Viking always has and always will be his nickname. Once the window was lowered all the way down, he was able to see the grinning red-haired man from the bar. Ominously, the man revved the vehicle's powerful engine. His right hand squeezed the steering wheel so tightly that his knuckles were white. Nicholas could

130

feel Lynn pushing backwards in his frame, as if she was trying to move away from the man. Buggleport's son apparently didn't get enough of a beating last time, because he asked Nicholas how the dead girl was inside him.

Before Nick could step forward and bash the guy's teeth down his throat, the car jumped forward fifteen feet and the headlights came on again. In front of them, the woods came alive. The dense trees appeared to move in segments, but as Nick's eyes adjusted to the light, he could see that they were actually not moving at all. There was an ocean of shadows watching them. Lynn pushed against Nicholas this time with enough force to knock him down on his derrière. He bounced up immediately as she pleaded with him to run. Lynn shrieked so loudly, he thought it blew out his eardrum. The shadows charged from the woods like an army storming the beaches of Normandy. To Nicholas's left stood young Buggleport, a few feet away from the car's open door. Although Nick never heard the car door open, the man was there smoking and still grinning his obnoxious smile just the same.

The two lovers were clearly pitted in a life and death struggle. Good judgment told them to run away from the entire situation. The car had obviously been placed there with the intention of raising false hopes, and not for an actual escape. But as the two looked at their alternatives and saw the shadows closing in fast and in large numbers, they went for the vehicle. For some reason, the man didn't try to stop them; he simply stepped out of the way like an accommodating doorman at a luxurious hotel. Nicholas jumped in and snapped the car into gear, the tires screeching as he headed off into the night. Behind them, the sound of hundreds of feet stopped all at once, as if they were commanded by a higher power. Buggleport's evil spawn wore his wretched smile for the last time that night, but it wasn't by the hand of Nicholas that he died. As the car drove away, the Rippers faded away into the shadows, and as they did so, the man's body fell lifelessly to the ground. He was no longer needed, so the Ripper inside joined the others in their search for humans to manipulate and eventually kill. The man's real name was Xavier Alan Buggleport. He took great pride in knowing that his father murdered for pleasure by commanding Rippers to do his deeds. Xavier was a man of sinister beginnings whose death was just reward for how he lived his life.

Many years ago, his father's Rippers had killed an innocent woman in her home. Her name was Eleanor Strude. Xavier never knew her when she was alive, but she saw him before her death. And after her death, when her shadow was cast as a Ripper, her Compatible happened to be

Xavier. Shadows exist all over the planet, yet out of all of those possible Compatibles, she was lucky enough to find him.

Eleanor lived in a small house that she had recently purchased in a historic district of town. The house was beautiful, but she never felt totally safe. At first she intended to try and ignore the noises, but when the noises became physical, she wanted to leave. One day she packed her personal belongings, intending to never return. She made it as far as the front door when the Rippers revealed themselves, sealing her fate. Her body was discovered days later, twisted and broken at the bottom of her basement stairs, a packed bag still in her hand.

When she connected with Xavier, her human thoughts returned, allowing her to execute a plan against him. Eleanor's death was unfortunate in the same way that Lynn's was. Nevertheless, Lynn lived a good life and came back as a Faith Finder, whereas Eleanor lived a good life and came back as a Ripper. But both women would get the vengeance they sought. The odd thing was that they retaliated against the same family. That goes to show that what comes around does go around.

Nicholas was now having the ride of his life, and he wasn't operating the devil's car as he thought earlier. He was reaching speeds of ninety miles per hour in his new car. In his pocket he still had the pile of money given to him by Patrick Conley. His new concern was to figure out why a guy who wanted him dead gave him a car instead. Lynn had no clue as to why, but the two of them knew something was screwed up. Nicholas thought that maybe he was taking the bait by taking the car. Perhaps he'd become too wrapped up in his problems to notice a trap. He slowed the car down as he approached a busier section of the city where flashing signs invited customers. There, in the road in front of them, was an accident of epic proportions. As Nicholas cruised closer, he could see that there were six vehicles involved. One man was lying on a stretcher, screaming that he had two broken legs. Paramedics and law enforcement personnel were trying to control the tragic scene. Three people were pronounced dead at the scene. The sheets draped over them were soaked through with blood, indicating that they were either dismembered or horribly gashed open. Others had injuries that were not life threatening but were very painful, as Nicholas and Lynn could see. The man who was screaming about his legs appeared to be going into shock. He kept apologizing for swerving his vehicle, but he said that there were dark figures in the road that looked like people. From where Nicholas's vehicle was positioned in traffic, the man's voice was clearly audible. He knew that he heard the man correctly. The man screamed once again that he was sorry, but there were shadowy figures and they were everywhere.

Lynn heard what Nicholas heard and suggested that they get out of town so as not to endanger anyone close to them, though she couldn't remember anyone's name offhand. Her memory was disappearing faster than ever. Nicholas drove to Doc Anderson's house to gather a few items for their journey. He had a creeping feeling that once he got there, he wasn't going to like what he found. Unfortunately, his premonition was correct. The road looked the same, but the house wasn't there. Trees that were once strong and healthy were now leafless and dead. Lynn asked him if he was sure he was on the same street. Had he taken a wrong turn? He didn't respond.

Nicholas drove with his mouth open, hanging on to the steering wheel like an old granny driving twenty in a sixty-five zone. The house had not been burned down or destroyed; it appeared to have never been built. In its place was a house that resembled a barn. A garbage truck was parked in the driveway. Out front was a mailbox that looked polished. On the box there was a name or acronym stenciled on the side that read "LETT." The mailbox seemed to be the only thing on the street that wasn't dreary or old. Nicholas didn't want to bring on another attack, so he stayed in the car. He tried honking the horn, but it didn't work. So he reached out the window with his left hand, grasped the handle on the mailbox door, and began opening it and closing it to try and get attention of anyone who might be around on the empty street.

After opening and closing the mailbox twenty or thirty times, a man opened the front door of the barn-style house. By the looks of him, they probably should have driven away immediately. He was about six feet tall and wore blue zip-up overalls, the kind garbage men wear. He was equipped with a garbage can lid covering his right shoulder and a large handgun in his left hand. "I suggest you put your vehicle in park," the man said. Seeing the barrel of the man's gun, Nicholas thought it would be wise to comply. The man walked down the steps with the gun pointed at Nicholas. "Are you in the habit of touching other men's mailboxes?" When Nick tried to explain, the man told him to shut up. "I ought to pump your pretty customized car full of lead."

Like a soldier going before a commanding officer to be reprimanded, Nicholas asked, "Permission to speak?" He was granted permission. Nicholas stuck both hands out the window to show that he was unarmed, also exposing his studded bracelet, black rubber band, arm scar, and tattoo. "Mr. Lett, I wonder if you could please tell me where Dr. Reid Anderson's house is located. It was here in the morning, but gone now."

The odd man stepped backwards, lowered the trash can lid, and spun his weapon around like a cowboy, holstering it in a cooking glove that was hanging from his rope belt. Nicholas thanked him for putting the big gun away.

After his drawn-out introduction, he introduced himself as Theodore Lett. "I've lived in this house since I was a tiny boy."

"Is this 212 Gavillion Parkway?"

"None other."

To say that Nicholas was at a loss for words would be an understatement. As he sat there, the man never even blinked; he only stared, smacking his gums at a tremendously irritating rate of speed. The good thing was he did have a shadow of his own. Lynn was kind enough to point this cause for optimism out to Nicholas to lighten the mood a bit. Theodore Lett said he owned his own independent garbage company called "Swill and Stuff." The name was on the side of the truck, and the truck was stinking like it was full of dead bodies. Nicholas didn't ask about the contents.

"Since the fella you're asking about doesn't live here, you must want your bag of junk. Or do you want me to dump it?" the man asked Nicholas. "A few years ago I had to replace the pipes in the yard. While I was digging, I kept coming across these small plastic screw-top containers filled with various items, photos and stuff. After I put my gun away here, I noticed that you resemble the person in the photos."

Nicholas's memory was definitely being erased, and so was Lynn's. He decided to appeal to the man's generous nature. "Would you mind reburying the items, as a favor from one gun collector to another?" Nick did not collect guns, but the small falsehood worked. "Maybe I'll come back one day to claim my stuff." It didn't make sense, but both of their memories were fading fast, so Nicholas wrote the man's name and address on one of his hundred-dollar bills. He totally had no recollection of burying anything anywhere. He may have done so and then mysteriously forgotten about it. Nicholas suspected that he and Lynn were in the middle of something else now, a situation that might well be more unexplainable and complicated than before.

For the man's troubles, Nick gave him a one-hundred-dollar bill. He looked very grateful as Nicholas shook his hand. The man said that if in the future his mailbox slams more than five times, he'll answer the door without his gun. Nick thanked the man and drove off once again. These times can try men's souls—that is, if souls exist as something other than shadows. The tired Viking believed that if an insane garbage man with a powerful handgun can shine some light on the day, then maybe there is hope.

Shadow Chapter
NUMBER
Twelve...

Nick and Lynn were now quickly driving away from the address where Reid Anderson apparently never lived. The house definitely did not look the same as it had earlier that day, before Nicholas left for work. Even though the address was the same and it was located on the same side of town and in exactly the same location, Reid's house simply wasn't there anymore.

While he drove, Nicholas started reminiscing about an old scheme that he'd never gotten the chance to put into action: his plan for a series of visits to prisons and insane asylums to conduct shadow research. Many innocent people had been convicted of crimes and murders that shadows were actually responsible for. And these innocent people would not be able to prove their innocence until the existence of shadows was revealed as proven fact. After watching that poor man in the accident with the broken legs put the blame on the shadows, Nick had a new motivation to work for the cause. Nicholas and Lynn had attempted to create a system of rules and regulations, without any results, unfortunately. Since the rules they made didn't always work, they needed a backup, a contingency plan, a way to get to the next step of whatever it was they were working through. So Nick decided they would head to Indiana to find Conrad Buggleport.

Driving eight hundred miles to face a murderer who controls an army of shadows was a simple plan. But in his current frame of mind, he had no fear of the unknown. In the eyes of an eighteen-year-old heading toward an unknown destination, the highway seemed endless. Every turn and twist revealed new scenery; license plates changed with each new state they entered. As you travel farther away from your home, thought Nicholas, people's facial features seem different. In Rhode Island, dark hair and dark features are common, but less so out west or down south where more light-colored hair is seen. This was fine with Nicholas, just in case he had to camouflage himself by blending in with a crowd. He hoped that there were also many tall people in Indiana. A state of midgets wouldn't give him room to hide. Nicholas had three other features that might give him away as a stranger. One was his strong Rhode Island accent. At four different gas stations along the way, people commented on how he left off consonants when he spoke. They'd compliment his fancy car, but then notice the two Rhode Island license plates; they were the second give-away. If they could have heard him silently yelling to every one watching that he was a Yankee, that would be a third.

One man in particular stuck out in Nicholas's mind. He was pumping gas into a tan 1970s Duster with plastic louvers and a homemade bra dangling from the front grill. He was leaning against the car with a hand on the hood while he stared in Nicholas's direction. Out of curiosity, Nick gave him a sidelong glance. "Hey, big guy," the man hollered over, "that Buick fits you like a glove." Nick grinned weakly and waved, fastening his gas cap kind of awkwardly and tighter than usual. He had no idea what to make of the stranger's statement or the somewhat sinister smile on his face. When Nicholas sat back in the car, he immediately told Lynn to shut up. He could feel her laughter building up inside him. She then let out a very loud chuckle, causing his face to turn a bright shade of red. He was unable to conceal his embarrassment. Lynn then informed him that for some reason, she wasn't jealous this time, not like she was at the bar when the girls hit on him. Nick replied with a sarcastic whatever. He burned rubber as he peeled away back to the highway.

After they took the Buick from Xavier Buggleport, Nicholas thought he saw the man fall dead to the ground moments later. He hadn't mentioned it to Lynn or asked her impression of the scene. He was too worried that she may have forgotten more stuff, like people's names or other things that took place along the way. His questions about Xavier Buggleport would have to take a backseat to their current situation. The young Viking was absolutely sure that all of his friends were not dead or missing. It sounded insane, but maybe they'd become temporarily transparent to him, or maybe they'd relocated for a purpose he did not know. If he found out that Earth was now Neptune or Mars or Venus, let it be. Nothing was shocking anymore. So he had to believe they were all alive and well, functioning normally.

To keep their minds occupied while they drove, Nick and Lynn tried to picture their lives ten years into the future. He would be twenty-eight when that time came. Nicholas wondered how their bond would hold up over the course of a decade. At that point in their lives, they would have history together reaching back twenty years.

He pulled the car off to the side of the road on eastbound highway 70, just before starting the final leg of their trip. Lynn suggested he relax and try to calm his nerves. Nicholas agreed. Her idea was top on his list, next to taking a leak. Considering it was only about fifty meters from the main road, the spot they parked in was secluded. By the look of the sky, it was early. According to the car's trip odometer, they'd covered 673 miles. Where they were was safe from swerving drunk drivers or questioning police officers. After Nicholas relieved himself in the bushes, he shut the engine off and reclined in the driver's seat. For the moment, he felt hidden behind the tinted black windows and the bandana that he'd slid down over his eyes.

Nicholas, somewhat sarcastically and jokingly, asked Lynn, "Are you ready to argue, maybe break the tension?"

She laughed. He always loved to hear her laugh. With equal sarcasm, she said, "Sure, why not."

"Why do you think we're forgetting people? Why are people disappearing? And why don't people with shadows have shadows." As he asked these questions, he stretched lazily, not expecting any answers to explain these mysteries. Nick put one foot up on the dash and bent the other leg over the steering wheel.

"Things are changing now, and I can't tell you why just yet."

Nicholas didn't change his comfortable body position in the car. "Are you kidding around?" he asked from behind the bandana that half covered his face.

"Shadows have reasons that are outside of human understanding."

That statement alone caused him to throw the car door open and slam both boots on the ground. He stood up on the pavement and asked, "Shadows have reasons that you can't tell me? When will it be the right time to tell me? Maybe when I'm half dead or half alive like you?" To illustrate his next point as fully as possible, Nick reached into the car and flipped the headlights on. He walked around to the front of the car and slammed both fists on the hood. Nicholas then furiously punched his own chest, screaming out loud, "I don't have a frigging shadow! I am without a shadow. Lynn, do you hear me?" The Viking roared into the morning sky. Nicholas didn't stop there. "All of my closest friends, except for Jimmy Meideros and Donna McClennon, have no shadows either. They live on earth, eat food, drink water, and defecate, but when I see them, I see no shadow. Please speak, before I drive the car off of a cliff. This is not a good time to tell me that shadows have reasons outside of human understanding."

Nicholas reached into his jeans pocket and pulled out the black locket that was given to him by someone he no longer remembered. He drew his powerful arm back with every intention of throwing the keepsake into the woods. Lynn screamed, "Please stop, Nicholas. Please don't do it. If you part with the locket, we will be separated forever." The desperate shadow girl blurted out, "I need you more than you need me." Lynn pleaded and begged, trying to avoid what was possibly the end. "I agree. Your rage is understandable. But you need to see that your patience, the patience I'm constantly talking about, has brought us far enough to unite our worlds. I never meant to deceive you, but

Conrad Buggleport will try and convince you that religions lied. Religions never lied. They simply did not know what was out there. That truth is for us to prove, don't you understand?"

Viking lowered his mighty hand, still holding the locket, and sat on the hood of the car. Lynn continued. "Your friends are fine. They are in a place where tomorrow ends and today begins here on earth. The only difference is that they are cut off from us as we are from them. Many powers are assisting us, powers of inestimable proportion, and they are colliding with dark powers that do not agree with our crusade. You and I have gone further than any human-shadow connection has ever gone. And we'll remain together forever, just as the name Nicholas Johansson will be remembered forever. You will be remembered as a leader and a Master of Faith, a faith that will bring loved ones together and end the sadness brought on by death."

Nicholas kissed the locket and put it back around his neck. He stood there, staring blankly into the woods. Cars were passing with greater frequency than they were earlier, as travelers headed to their destinations. Nick opened and closed his hands and wiggled his fingers around to keep them from swelling.

"Lynn, I love you, but I'm only human. My mortal heart can't take much more. I feel like I'm in the process of losing my life. And all I have to show for it is a bunch of things buried in plastic containers in some nut job's backyard in an alternate world."

Nicholas looked down and noticed the front license plate. It said VKNG-B37. B37 was the number of the hospital room he stayed in after he was injured as a kid. He thought it was odd that humorous things happened even in alternate worlds. Maybe it was him, and just that he had a strange sense of humor. Or possibly the powers that be knew what buttons to push to get him to complete the job.

Nicholas retied his bandana and got back in the car. He started rummaging through the glove box in search of a map. Nick figured if this world had gas stations and a sense of humor, why not a map to figure it all out. He never asked for a shadow girlfriend or a free car or a big envelope of money, but he got those things. He didn't find a map, but he did find a large key that had circle with a cross through it etched into one side. Nicholas liked the looks of the target symbol on the key, so he added it to the chain that he had the locket on. He thought to himself that if he adds any more to that chain, he's going to start looking like Mr. T from *Rocky III*. He felt like saying "I pity the fool." Like Mr. T, Nick pitied the fool that got in his way.

"Are you okay to continue? Or do you want to ask more questions?"

Nicholas lowered the window, hocked up a loogie, and spit it out the window. It landed about twelve feet away, splattering on the already discolored, cracked pavement. "Say, did you know the Chinese guy who drove by in the green Subaru twenty minutes ago?"

"I don't remember seeing anyone."

"Things are really changing fast," Nicholas said.

"Why?"

"I saw that man plus his female shadow inside."

"That's impossible. You could never see that."

Nick didn't argue. He just smirked, acknowledging to himself that he definitely saw what he saw, despite what she didn't see.

The wheels of the Buick were spinning, once again catching pavement as they accelerated onto the highway. After several hours of driving, they finally crossed over into Indiana and stopped at a gas station called The Mark. At the counter there was a sign that said free maps. They'd passed a highway sign that said it was seventy miles to Indianapolis, so Nicholas was going to disregard the free maps, but Lynn said he should take one just in case.

Nick completely unfolded the map on a table in the gas station. The first thing he noticed was the aerial view of Indianapolis itself. It looked like a giant target, like the one etched on the key that he'd found in the glove box of the car. The circle was a highway called I-465. The one they were on was I-70, and the one heading roughly north and south was I-74. Together they created the clue that corresponded to the markings on his key. The map took a little imagination to picture an actual target from the squiggly lines but threw exhausted eyes they symbolized hope. Nicholas removed the chain from his neck to examine the key more closely. He located a small pinpoint scratch near the target that looked as if it had been deliberately placed there. According to the map, the closest point matching the location of the scratch was a town called New Palestine. Nicholas asked the old man at the counter, a man without a shadow, if he'd ever heard of the town.

The man said in a long, drawn-out way, "Well, it's one of those small towns with one streetlight surrounded by cornfields. Throughout the cornfields there's long stretches of road leading to communities of country folk. Have you ever been to a small town, young man?" "Rhode Island is as small as it gets, mister." The man behind the counter was so polite that Nick felt like a jerk asking his next question. He thanked the man for the map. With a big friendly smile, the man asked if he could help him with anything else. Trying to be nonchalant, Nicholas asked, "Well, I'm curious. How long have you been without a shadow?"

The gentleman's smile disappeared, but his facial expression wasn't angry. "Asking folks personal questions that can't be answered is rude. Questions like that lead to other questions, eventually hurting people's feelings. In the long run, it's better to leave the unexplainable unexplained."

Nicholas was more than a little spooked by Farmer Brown's response. The fact that the man called his lack of a shadow unexplainable was odd. That must mean he has no memory of connecting with the shadow in the first place. Perhaps in this alternate world, being without a shadow is the equivalent of having a disability or a strange birthmark or mole on the end of your nose. Either way, Nicholas welcomed more exhausted driving after the stimulating discussion with the old man at the counter.

Once back in the car, Nick slurped down a Coke, trying to take in as much caffeine as he could handle in order to stay awake. He was so incredibly tired that he couldn't remember if he'd paid for it or not. If he had, the man at the counter made out like a champ, because Nick had no new loose change in his pocket, just more one-hundred-dollar bills. If he hadn't, the man would definitely label him the rude Rhode Island drifter who asks mean questions and steals soda.

According to the map, New Palestine wasn't very far away, at least not in comparison to the eight hundred miles they'd already traveled. Before the trip, Nicholas had worked seven hours of his scheduled ten-hour shift at Conley's Bar. He'd fought off three good-sized Rippers with human Compatibles and was later chased by an army of Rippers. Nicholas saw a man drop dead in the street, and last, but not least, he was almost shot in the head by an insane garbage man with a really nice mailbox. After all of that, a shower and a bed would be priceless, he thought to himself.

A few miles up the road was a turnoff with a wooden sign that said hotel. It was very old, with no paint, just stained clapboards that were mostly falling off of the structure. The room doors appeared to be custom made. They had huge keyholes to go along with their large arched style. Nick and Lynn parked the Buick four spots away from the main door to the hotel. The rear of the hotel was totally surrounded by woods, from what they could see. Before getting out of the car, he asked Lynn, "Please keep your eyes peeled, because whatever could happen, will."

"I'll stay alert," she said, "but you'll be safe at this particular hotel."

"Why is that? Is this a place that somehow you've been before?"

Lynn explained, "Behind the hotel there's a historical cemetery called The Grace of Florence. In this world, my vision has 360-degree capability. I saw another sign that you missed on the way in. While you were looking straight ahead, concentrating on the crooked road, I noticed it off to the left, half covered by trees. Would you like to know how a cemetery can provide protection from Rippers?"

He yawned and said, "Another explanation is not needed at the current moment, but a bed certainly is."

Suddenly their attention was diverted by the sound of familiar music from both of their pasts. Nicholas got out of the car to listen more closely. The blaring music was the hard, drum-bashing, guitar-smashing sound of Puppet Crotch, which, as it turned out, happened to be their favorite band. But Nicholas hadn't known until now that his Shadow Princess enjoyed speed metal in her former life. Nicholas whacked his open palm flat on the roof of the car. "Do you recognize the tunes?"

"It's definitely album number three's 1987 release of 'Meat Dancers.' The album was released under the name *Brainwashed Human Junk* by the ultimate speed metal band, Puppet Crotch."

Nicholas was slightly shocked to learn that she knew this music, music that he loved. Then he said, accusingly, "Wait a minute. You've been reading my mind, haven't you? You aren't a metal head like I am. You're just attempting to agree to look cool, that's all."

"No, I'm afraid not. My mind-reading capability is now totally gone. It started to leave me not long after we entered this alternate world, for your information. Say, do you know who Davie John Vitta is?" Nicholas crinkled his face in confusion and said that the name wasn't familiar. "He wrote the original version of the song before Puppet Crotch was even hatched from their mamas. If you really rocked, you would know that sort of stuff. My past, I mean, what happened before I was murdered, is clearer than ever now. When I was fourteen, I went to a Puppet Crotch concert. At the concert, I bought one of their T-shirts and wore it until it fell apart. It became so tattered and thin, I made it into a sleeveless shirt, then a sleeveless half shirt. Eventually the logo was unrecognizable, so hanging it on the bedroom wall so I could savor the experience was all that it was good for."

Her voice sounded free as she told the story. It was a shame that they were losing each other, Nicholas thought. This world was peeling them apart from some of their memories and also dissolving their bond. They laughed together as if a good-bye was on the horizon. Neither of them hinted to the other about the feeling, because the moment was too great to ruin.

Together, mortal man and shadow woman, they walked toward the front door of the hotel. The name on the door was Florence's Inn. Lynn wondered to herself if the lady owned the cemetery too, or was it an odd coincidence? She would soon get her answer. When the door opened, they were greeted by a tiny woman, no taller than four feet ten. She walked right up to Nicholas, looking up in the sky to see his face. The woman introduced herself as Florence, which answered Lynn's question about the cemetery.

"Is the room for you alone," Florence asked, "or will your beautiful lady friend be staying the night as well?"

"Why can I not see some people's shadows, like the guy at the counter in the gas station, but I can see yours?"

She smiled. "Not everyone who receives a gift reaps the same rewards. We're each special in our own way. So, does Lynn keep on you to be patient every now and again?"

He nodded north and south with his mouth hanging open.

"You're on the path of greatness, you know, and you're being led by a shadow woman with a pure heart."

"Holy crap!" Nicholas couldn't help himself. He didn't even know he'd said it. It just leaked out of his mouth. All these predictions came from this little lady, and only a few seconds after opening the front door.

"I've got the gift of reading shadows," Florence said, "especially ones who've found the perfect Compatible, like you." She then changed the subject. "The cemetery behind the building was named after my grandmother five generations ago. Do the two of you feel safe?" Nicholas and Lynn said yes and simultaneously followed Florence into the building.

"I assure you, I would never answer the door if I expected an evil person to be standing there to greet me." The kind little lady took Nicholas's giant hand and led him into the kitchen, where she prepared a meal fit for a Viking. Nicholas consumed three plates of food while he and Lynn carried on a conversation with the nice lady. Their talk was very enjoyable. It felt like they were sitting in three individual seats, for Florence could speak with Lynn freely, without telepathic communication, and Lynn could do the same. Nicholas didn't count Florence's shadow, because he couldn't see her shadow, nor did her shadow attempt to communicate with either of them. After dinner, the food worked like a tranquilizer in the digestive tract of the already sleepy giant.

"How much do I owe you for the meal and the room?" Nicholas asked.

"Dinner is on the house, and your room key is around your neck, next to the lovely locket with Lynn's picture inside. Checkout time is whenever you wake up, since you're probably exhausted and need the rest. I wonder, though," the kind woman said, "if would you be interested in meeting some of my friends at a later time?"

Nicholas said yes.

"If you're lucky, they'll play some more of that music that you heard when you pulled up to the hotel. My friends also may be able to shine some light from a different direction on your situation."

Sleep was only footsteps away, and Nicholas's mind was cluttered to the max with questions about everything. How did Florence know that he called her Lynn when her real name is Monica Lamestra? During the time that he'd been around Florence, he never even spoke Lynn's name once. And she knew about the locket, the key, and all their business, and she even had a Puppet Crotch CD. In any case, her hospitality was unbelievable. The key fit the lock, just like the lady said, and with one turn the door was open. Nicholas saw the bed on the other side of the spotless hotel room. It looked like a distant oasis playing mind games with a dying man. As he drew closer, he noticed a plate next to the bed filled with peanut butter and walnut cookies. Beside that was a tall glass of milk. He fell asleep with a milk mustache and a cookie in his hand.

Shadow Chapter
NUMBER
Thirteen...

Fourteen hours he slept. Fourteen hours filled with screaming dreams and uncontrollable nightmares that made his exhausted body twitch and contort as he tried to rest. Finally, the sleeping Viking awoke. For awhile he just lay there, his eyes focused on the swirling pattern of the textured ceiling. His sheets were soaked, and they reeked with the stench of perspiration. He sat up, feeling stiff, despite the comfortable mattress. Nicholas moaned loudly as he cracked his back. As he got up to go to the bathroom for his morning duty, he noticed that Florence had left him clothes and toiletries on the table across from the bed. Next to the stack was a piece of paper folded in four sections, along with the locket and key. He imagined that Florence must have found the key sticking out of the room door after he stumbled into bed. Nicholas scratched himself and said to Lynn that he must've been totally wrecked last night to forget that.

Nicholas took a shower, washing off two days of sweat and caked-on grime. He then put on the clothes Florence left for him on the table. They were such a perfect fit that they felt like they were straight from his closet back in Rhode Island. Nick wondered how Florence found an XXL sweatshirt and T-shirt out of the blue. Even the pants were a 34/38 and slightly faded, just the way Nick liked to wear them. She'd never even asked for his size. He stuffed all of his stinking dirty clothes inside the jeans that he'd been wearing and tied the legs over the top, securing the entire package like a small duffle bag. Before putting the necklace back on, he admired the key with the target scratched in it. He then put the locket back around his neck and tucked it under his new shirt.

To thank Florence for her hospitality, Nicholas stripped the bed and cleaned up the bathroom a bit. Hotels are normally professionally cleaned, but he felt thankful for his comfortable stay and the absence of roaches, so he thought why not. Nick walked back to the table where he'd found the new clothes and unfolded the piece of paper that was lying there. It was written in calligraphy and said, "Four eyes are better than two, so please join us in the main lobby for a snack and an explanation."

He asked Lynn what she thought of the odd note, but there was no answer. He called her name several more times, but still no answer. Nicholas couldn't believe that she was gone. His body began to feel different, as if a piece of him was suddenly missing or taken by a thief in the night. The note in his hand had to be leading him to his ultimate fate. He spun around in the room to see if Rippers were already on his tail, since without Lynn he was easily open to their attacks.

Nicholas had just begun scanning every inch of the room, when there was a hard knock at the door behind him. The boy jerked the door open so fast, he surprised the man and woman in hotel uniforms who stood there ready to greet him. Neither of them looked like the Grim Reaper or a mad killer hunting him down. They took the liberty of introducing themselves before Nicholas had time to speak. Joe was a big burly guy with a kind face. Melissa also had a kind face and resembled Jamie Gertz from the Vampire movie *The Lost Boys*. Nick swung his bundle of dirty clothes over his shoulder and stepped out the door. He showed Joe and Melissa the note and asked if they had any idea what it meant, but instead of answering his question, they kept their friendly smiles and walked away toward the main lobby. Nicholas reluctantly followed them. He had a sour feeling in the pit in his stomach from nervousness and a pain in his heart from missing the feeling of Lynn inside him.

As he entered through the door of the hotel lobby, his eyes fell upon a gorgeous woman sitting at a large oval table. She was wearing a black gothic dress that matched the color of her hair. Her skin was slightly pale, like that of a porcelain doll, but her features were seductive and alluring. She stood and introduced herself as Roslyn. Roslyn then said that she has been chosen as the one for him. The woman signaled with a hand gesture for him to join her at the table. But Nicholas did not move a muscle. He stood there in the doorway until Florence, Joe, and Melissa sat down with Roslyn. A lit scented candle sat on the table in front of each person. A fifth, unlit candle sat in front of an empty chair. It was obviously intended for Nick. He closed the door behind him and approached the table with a great deal of apprehension. He took a few paces toward them and, holding up the note, demanded to know where Lynn was. His red face and sweaty forehead displayed how seriously he felt about receiving an answer to his question. Florence could see his level of aggravation, so she walked over to the angry Viking and hugged him. Despite Nick's flaming temper, he hugged the tiny woman back and then joined them at the table. As soon as he was seated, the candle in front of him magically lit itself. After staring at it for a few seconds, Nicholas looked up and again asked the group to tell him where Lynn was.

Florence smiled. "Did you enjoy your stay, Nicholas?" she asked.

"I had a great time. Thank you for the food and clothes, and thank you for your hospitality. But I want to find Lynn and get back on the road, if that's okay?" His patience was growing thinner by the second as his concern for Lynn grew.

Melissa, the hotel staff girl, spoke up. "Nicholas, I wonder if I might tell you a quick story? It will explain to you where Lynn has gone temporarily."

Nick looked at her and asked, "Why didn't you speak up sooner?"

"Joe, who is sitting across from you, was once a shadow on my wall. I allowed him to join with me, just as you did with Lynn. As the years passed, we grew closer. Eventually we were offered the gift of reincarnation. Reincarnation involves a spiritual trade from one Faith Finder to another and one mortal to another. To be reincarnated, Joe had to join with another mortal, and that mortal's shadow had to join with me. Moreover, each new connection destroys one Ripper connection. When a Ripper connection is broken, the human involved dies and the Ripper shadow is gone forever. Lynn tells us that when you left Rhode Island, Xavier Buggleport died in the street." Nicholas nodded his head in agreement as he nervously played with his black rubber band under the table. "Xavier died because a connection was made somewhere else in the world, putting an end to his pathetic existence."

Joe extended his hand across the table toward Nicholas. They shook hands, and then Nick politely asked to hear his story.

"Let me begin by saying that I've never been happier. I am now a cross between what I was then and what I am now."

"What the hell is that supposed to mean?" Nicholas asked Joe. "Do you mean you changed figuratively, or literally?"

"A perfect connection leads you through a long series of tests, as I imagine you're already aware. The tests are in place to see if your connection has what it takes to cross over from body to body. The crossover changes you slightly, allowing another to live again. Merging has not always been possible. Only a select few have been able to complete the process. Once complete, it does slightly alter the appearance and personality of a person. The change is a permanent sacrifice to help another."

As the conversation went on, Florence listened silently. But now it was her turn to speak. "I'm worried, Nicholas, about how you will react to such a strange concept. You asked yesterday about the shadows people have and sometimes don't have. My explanation may confuse your mind even more. You see, I, Florence Grace, am an angel, as is Donna McClennon, Reid Anderson's mother. Yesterday I told you that not everyone who receives a gift reaps the same rewards, that each of us is special in our own way. I, for example, am a protector of shadows who cross human partners to connect. Donna, on the other hand, is a protector of humans with shadows inside, though she does not know that. She is not able to see any shadows other than the one she casts on the wall. Her physical shadow and my shadow," Florence continued, "are the few in this story that have scientific explanations for their appearance."

Nicholas asked Florence, "Who does the Puppet Crotch CD belong to?" Melissa said that it was hers. "It would calm my nerves if I could listen to it," Nicholas said. Joe got up and went in the other room to put the music on. Things immediately got weird when Nicholas asked Roslyn to tell her story now. "Basically," Roslyn said, "my story is almost the same as Joe and Melissa's, but it revolves around you." She pointed at Nicholas and slid an envelope over to Melissa for her to pass his way. Inside the envelope were three photos. One was a photo of Lynn when she was alive. The second was a photo taken the day before of a girl who looked almost exactly like Roslyn. The third photo was of a woman who appeared to be a combination of Lynn and the girl in the second photo. The woman in third photo looked identical to Roslyn sitting before him. It took a minute for this to register in Nicholas's mind. As he sat silently staring at the picture, Roslyn asked Nicholas if he liked how they looked. Nicholas slid the pictures back across the table and stood up. He appeared to be hurt, almost as if he'd been betrayed. In the background, the CD was playing a song called "Dangling Strings." It came on like theme music would in a movie or show. It seemed preplanned, but it didn't set the stage for what was about to take place.

"Could I speak to Lynn?" Nicholas asked.

"Not yet," Roslyn replied, "but soon you'll be able to."

"I want to know how I will change if I merge. And who's going to merge with me? Mainly, I want to know if I'll remember Lynn. If I do, will the feelings be mine or a combination?"

Roslyn's face saddened because of the answer she had to give him. "The picture in the locket," she said, "will become meaningless after the connection. You'll only remember Lynn as a shadow that was once on your wall when you were a child." Speaking to the group, Roslyn said, "Lynn wants you to know that she would rather be nonexistent than lie to the man she loves. That is why I am telling you this." Roslyn began sobbing deeply. "My tears," she explained, "are for the one I lost. He was once inside me, waiting to connect with Nicholas to merge as one being. If the connection begins, as it has between me and Lynn, it must go all the way, otherwise both shadows are lost forever. If you do not merge with him, my shadow will never be seen again. The same fate awaits Lynn; she cannot go back to you or stay with me if you do not merge.

Nicholas was furious. "This took place without my permission. I feel cheated and lied to. I'm about to be transformed into something I do not care to be. How, I want to know, did Reid and Donna conveniently appear in my life? And what about Brian and Zack?" Before anyone could answer, he rambled on hysterically. "I was set up from the beginning. My accident, my parents' death, the shadow attacks, the job at Conley's Bar, the envelope of money, the free car to travel to Indiana ..."

Florence told him to stop and listen. "You were not set up at all. You were chosen by both sides, Faith Finder and Ripper. And you were great, even as a young man. Your high level of strength, both physical and mental, is equal to your compassion and loyalty. These traits were evident at the age of eight, when you stepped out into the cold to protect your family. You acted with no regard for your own life. That moment," Florence said, "was only the beginning for you and Lynn, but it spelled the end of the Rippers' efforts to join you as one, for they search for evil, not good. In the world you are in now, you will have to sacrifice more than you ever did in the past. And you will have to be willing to sacrifice for another whom you have never met. And," she added mysteriously, "you've made it to the five points of light."

"If I decide not to join, will I be considered a killer? Nicholas asked.

"Not in the physical sense," Melissa replied, "but in other ways, you would be stopping a life from regenerating, so yes."

"I have two final questions to ask before I make my decision. First, I want to know if Conrad Buggleport will die if I unite with Roslyn."

Joe said, "Honestly, there is no guarantee. One Ripper-mortal connection will definitely end, but knowing the individuals involved is impossible."

"My second question is this: in the alternate world to this one, are my parents and friends alive or dead?"

Florence replied to this question. "Nicholas, you are a man of honor torn in two directions. One side of you knows what is tangible and real. The other knows what is in your heart." Nicholas believed every word she said. "Basically," she said, "the decision is yours."

The table before him was full of genuine people devoted to helping a cause. If that meant altering their own natural-born selves to complete what they felt was necessary, then that's what they had to do. Nicholas could see by the look on Florence's face and her response to his last question that she never had a choice of her own. She'd been placed here as an angel to be a part of the hotel and the peaceful cemetery behind it.

Nicholas knew now that he didn't have to kill Conrad Buggleport. Buggleport was an evil man who thrived on murder to fill his empty heart. It's easy to be evil, Nicholas thought to himself. Souls do exist, if you choose to identify them. A soul doesn't only have to be noticed after the person is dead; if you can see it while it's here, you've allowed it to live forever.

Nicholas took Lynn's locket off of his neck for the last time. He asked Florence, "Is Lynn buried behind the hotel in your family's graveyard?"

Seeing that Nicholas was going to leave, Roslyn interrupted. "Please, Nicholas, don't let their shadows die."

He did not respond; he just waited for Florence's response.

"Her grave is the one near the tree," Florence said. "The orphanage in Rhode Island thought that it would be nice to send her home after her death to be buried where she was born. Monica Lamestra was of Spanish decent. Her parents originally came to the United States and made Indiana their home. I'm honored to have the final resting place of the innocent girl among my loved ones." When Lynn was in Nicholas and together they arrived at the hotel in Indiana, however, she had no idea her remains were less than fifty meters away.

Nicholas put the locket across his chest and apologized to Roslyn for both of their losses. "The journey," he said, "isn't over for me yet or for you. If you look within yourself, the separation from the one you love inside will be temporary." Then, without excusing himself or saying good-bye, he left the key on the table and marched out the door with the locket still pressed against his chest.

Once outside, he stuck close to the perimeter of the hotel until he reached the gates of the graveyard. In the graveyard, many gravestones were worn illegible by erosion, but none of the graves was neglected. The grounds were impeccably cared for by someone's respectful hand. Near the tree that Florence described was the grave of Nicholas's Lynn, Monica Lamestra. Her small grave was marked with a flat horizontal stone that read: "Monica Lamestra—A girl that held the hearts of two worlds." The statement alone gave Nicholas chills. It was ironic that the words carved on her grave reflected the life she lived after death. He knelt at the stone, draping Lynn's locket over the top. He closed his eyes tightly and said a few words.

"Lynn," he began, "I am empty without you inside. I'm the man that I've become because of your involvement in my life. Imagining a life without memories of what we've had together is a life that I would not want to live. I'm sorry for letting everyone down by not joining with Roslyn and her shadow, but I feel there is more that needs to be done. If my life ends outside the gates of this cemetery, at least I'll die with the most beautiful vision that was ever granted to a mortal man,
the vision of the moments that I spent with you, Lynn."

Nicholas made his next decision with neither reluctance nor hesitation. He walked toward the gates, a proud man following his heart. As he approached the gates, he could see the Rippers gathering outside the crooked metal fence, knowing he was now alone and waiting for the attack. Most men, knowing that they were going to die, would cower in fear. Nicholas, on the other hand, couldn't stop laughing. He was picturing Lynn as a kid at that Puppet Crotch concert, rocking out in her new T-shirt. He remembered how she said that she hung it on the wall after she'd worn it too many times. It was all faded and cut in half, and it had holes and no sleeves, but she hung on to it until she had to let it go. Nicholas wasn't an old T-shirt, but he understood the concept of being at the end of his useful life. On his way out of the cemetery, he picked up a big rock to use for defense. As he got closer to the gate, however, he put it down and decided to go without a fight.

Many thoughts go through your mind when you're close to inevitable death. Unanswered questions magically become answered as your mind looks for solutions. Rippers surrounded every inch of the cemetery grounds. He sensed that they wanted him to die slowly and suffer. Nicholas still had options, options that he had no idea existed before he met Lynn or came to Indiana. When he dies, he may become an Angel or a Faith Finder, or he may peacefully rot in a box. There is always that chance he would become a Ripper or a Dormant, but who wants to think negative thoughts at a time like this. The odds are in his favor that things are going to go well in the after death.

As Nicholas passed through the gate, he closed his eyes and stepped into death's dark clutches. It was over quickly. And it proved to be as unsatisfying as any human could imagine. The pain was unspeakable. Excruciating and agonizing did not come close to describing it. The biggest shock, however, came when Nicholas awoke.

Shadow Chapter
NUMBER
Fourteen...

Waking up after being murdered? Say you drank poison, lit a stick of dynamite, and went parachuting without a parachute. Obviously this would leave you in a place where you wouldn't have the ability to tell the story later on. Nicholas Johansson used to think this way until something similar actually happened to him. The man had a round-trip ticket to hell and back. And he would return unscathed and breathing free air once again.

Nicholas couldn't imagine how it would feel to wake up a shadow. He did have an idea how it would feel to wake up cold and alone in a morgue lying among the silenced. All the lights were out when Nicholas opened his eyes under the perfectly draped sheet. It covered him almost entirely, exposing only his feet. He lay there on the uncomfortable, unpadded table like a pig on display at a buffet. His body was completely naked and freezing cold, as if all the blood had been drained from it. Under the sheet, his blurry vision was limited. He could move his eyes up and down but not left or right; it was as if his brain wasn't receiving the command. Through the sheet, however, he was able to see small, rectangular areas of light high on the wall that could possibly be windows. As he focused on trying to move his body, it seemed that nothing at all was responding. So he decided to put his energy into what he knew actually did work.

Nicholas could see, think, breathe, and feel the cold throughout his body. This was very positive, because he figured feeling the cold meant he wasn't paralyzed permanently. He wasn't a doctor, but his self-diagnosis was enough to calm his nerves temporarily. These limited functions would lead to other bodily responses if he remained patient.

His mind wandered toward self-pity. His feet felt like icicles. The table was so cold, it made clear thought impossible, but Nicholas knew that he had to hang on to hope. Watching the rectangular areas of light change made him feel better, if only for a short time. He was trying to blink as fast as he could to increase the space between the sheet and his eyelashes. The sheet barely nicked the tips of his eyelashes, but it was still extremely irritating. If he could have exchanged irritation for pain, he would have chosen pain at this point. A good smack in the head would be a welcome trade. The sheet smelled funny, and it had a stiff texture, as if it had been starched. Nicholas closed his eyes to try and concentrated on building up an inner warmth to kick start his body. He thought of Lynn when she pranced across the wall at the hospital. At that time, Nick was just a boy, all alone in a strange place for the first time, dealing with a head injury and a severe wound. He remembered that he felt many feelings at that time, but never did he feel like quitting. Quitting was not and would never be an option. Anger, despair, hatred, love, turmoil, exhaustion—these were in Nicholas's vocabulary. The Q word was not.

The young man opened his eyes. He was beginning to warm up from his inner fire. His eyes could now move left and right and around in a circle. Blinking and moving his eyes triggered partial facial movements. A nose twitch led to movement of his lips. A positive attitude ignited by hope was his fuel. All this time he was able to rationalize. Rationalization had kept him sane for all those years, as did having an understanding of his surroundings. The rectangles on the wall, he decided, were windows. When he realized that, he wanted to slap himself in the noodle for being so blind. However, he was as yet unable to move, so he would have to wait until later to abuse himself.

The room was filled with a sound, a repetitive sound that distinctly seemed to generate from inside of his head. Nicholas listened for a while to the incessant rattling sound. If he bit down hard, the sound ended, but doing so produced a scream. The sound, he now realized, was the chattering of his own teeth, and the scream was emitted by him when he accidentally bit his tongue in the process. "I screamed," Nicholas yelled out loud. He was now hollering and talking random nonsense from under the sheet, simply because he could. The sound of his voice echoed, as if he was in a cave. Nicholas blew out air from his cheeks in an attempt to create more space around his face. The sheet was still barely touching his eyelashes, and it was driving him nuts.

Suddenly he twitched. Then he twitched again, violently jerking his monstrous frame three inches off of the steel slab. Each twitch was more painful than the last, but at least nothing was touching his eyelashes anymore. After ten violent jerks, the episode ended. His body felt like it was being pricked by thousands of needles, both large and small.

A new sound presented itself in the room: the beating of his heart. It started banging inside his chest like a locomotive speeding down the tracks. Nicholas's body now warmed at a drastically increased rate. The series of bodily twitches left him lying on his right side in a fetal position as he began to regain feeling. His right hand was now close enough to reach his face. He didn't touch his face, however; he decided to feel the top of his head instead. In that position, he should have been able to see his bangs hanging down, but he couldn't. As his hand slowly investigated his cranium, it slid down to analyze his face, like a blind person reading Braille. All of his hair was completely gone, including his eyebrows and five o'clock shadow. Nicholas was still very weak. He used the same hand to check other parts of his body for any unexpected changes. As he thought, he was oddly hairless. His eyelashes were definitely intact, however, a fact he was well aware of thanks to the sheet.

The sheet was now half off of his body. In case someone was in the room watching Nicholas, he wanted to surprise them before they surprised him. He wanted his entrance back into the world of the erect and vertical to be shocking for all to see. As it happened, his entrance was more of a shock to him than anyone else. It's hard to be subtle when you're close to seven feet tall and pushing two hundred fifty pounds. The sheet flew one way like a kite in a windstorm, and Nicholas hit the floor like a piano falling out of a skyscraper window. The Viking was now on the floor, still naked but happy to have regained full movement.

As Nicholas rose to his feet, he was able to see the meaning of the sheet that was draped over him. The entire room was full of sheets, feet sticking out of them, each tagged at the toe. He stood still until he was able to get the entire scene into perspective. It all made him sick to his stomach. Nicholas thought that perhaps he should have stayed under the sheet a while longer. When he leaped off the table, his toe tag had fallen off and was lying under the sheet on the floor. Nick picked it up and checked the spelling of his name. Next to his name was that damn letter combination again, B37. First it showed up at the hospital, then on the license plate, and now here. People's reactions to things don't seem to change much as time passes. He remembered being eight years old at the hospital and studying his identification bracelet for mistakes. He was doing the same thing now, except his attention was on his own toe tag. At least if there was a mistake, he has the ability to correct it, unlike the other folks in the room.

Nicholas walked over to the rectangular windows. They were the first thing he'd noticed when he opened his eyes. It seemed that they were tinted. They were too small for a person to climb through, especially a person of his size. He picked up the sheet and made a quick toga out of it. His knot was a bit awkward, due to his hands being sore. It served its purpose, though, but resembled a giant diaper instead.

His journey down the corridor of feet and sheets was uncomfortable. At the end, around the corner, there was a row of cold chambers where dead bodies are stored, leading to a single office door. The door had a key pad system attached to it that required a code of some kind to open. It was charcoal gray with black tinted glass. The coloration reminded Nicholas of Lynn's description of her shadow world. Three-inch-high block letters on the door's nameplate spelled out the name MEIDEROS. Nicholas ran his finger over the letters in amazement. He wondered how the hell he'd ended up back in Rhode Island and in the morgue of his old buddy, Jimmy Meideros. When confused or aggravated, Nicholas normally grabbed his long bangs as a focus of concentration. Reid Anderson had told Nicholas how important it was to establish focal points. The man had meant a point to stare at, but Nicholas felt that the hair pulling worked best. He was now totally bald, so that was unfortunately out of the question for now. So he just rubbed his scalp instead. As he stared into the black glass of the office door, he realized that he could remember everything from his past as clearly as if it had happened yesterday.

He flipped the switch to the hall light, nearly scaring himself half to death. His body cast a shadow of its own on the wall behind him. It was a figure that he hadn't seen in years. Nicholas then realized that he'd been sent here by Florence. Either she'd given him a life again or sent him to the morgue to be safe from Rippers. He couldn't understand how he could be rewarded for not accepting the connection with Roslyn. Maybe this wasn't a reward but a steppingstone to something else. Nicholas turned to his shadow to test it, to see if it was his own. He waved his right hand then his left hand. Then he lifted one leg, accidentally losing his toga on the floor. He retied the sheet as he considered what to do next.

He had nothing else to do, so he wandered the halls of the underground morgue to see what he could see. Most of the rooms he passed were empty, until he reached room number four. The door, marked Laundry and Belongings, was secured with a padlock attached to a small cheap metal clasp, The kind of clasp you'd find on a basement door to a pantry. Nicholas needed clothes, so he held on to his toga and gave the door a swift straight kick. It fell easily, splintering all over the floor. The interior of the room resembled a Good Will or Salvation Army store, full of clothes and shoes belonging to the deceased. Nicholas started picking through the clothes trying to find his size. The search seemed endless and hopeless, but he kept looking until he found what he needed: black oil-resistant boots that fit perfectly, a comfortable pair of blue jeans that smelled clean, and an extra-large black T-shirt with a pocket in front. He even found a knit cap to cover his bald head. The hat was pretty cool. It was orange and black with embroidery on the front that said "Gash." He had no idea what that meant, but like the jeans, it smelled clean, so it was good to go. On his way out he found a nice navy P-coat that fit like it was tailor-made. Nicholas actually wanted to join the navy someday, so he thought that he might as well get adjusted to dressing like a sailor. A nice coat like this would also serve him well in case the weather outside was snowing or cold. Looking out the small window in the other room, he hadn't been able to determine the weather too well.

As Nicholas concluded his shopping spree, he pulled the long pink string attached to the light. His good deed to save energy was not rewarded well, for he ended up tripping over a piece of the broken door that was connected to a poorly setup alarm system. When he originally smashed the whole door in, it hadn't tripped the alarm. A little extra clumsiness was all it took. What idiot thought it would make sense to secure a laundry room located in a morgue? The alarm blared so loudly, it sounded like a fire truck was in the room. He frantically searched for the source of the wiring so he could disable it. The wire ran around the perimeter of the ceiling, but seemed to lead to nothing other than more wires. Then he thought he heard a door upstairs open and footsteps working their way down to investigate the disturbance.

Nicholas grabbed his sheet, trying to think of a place to hide. He ran as fast as he could back to the table that he'd awoken on a few rooms over. He started undressing as much as he could as he hustled down the hall. He stripped off the rest of his clothes and laid them flat on the table and between his legs. This way with the sheet over him, no one would notice at a glance that the body had ever been disturbed. Nicholas reacted to the sound of the upstairs door with split-second timing. Yet now that he was back under the sheet, he realized that the door to the laundry room was totally destroyed. He was also breathing very heavily, and dead people under sheets usually don't breathe at all.

The light snapped on in the room full of corpses that he was in. Nick listened to the footsteps. Someone walked in six or seven paces and then stopped suddenly. Nicholas panicked, hoping that his cover wasn't blown that easily. He couldn't turn his head to see what the person was doing, but he imagined that they were playing a game, the game of "one of these things is not like the other one." One thing was different, and it wasn't that he was alive and breathing. It was that he had no toe tag like the other quietly obedient dead people. His toe tag was on the floor. The shoes shuffled, stopped, and then shuffled again. Nicholas could now see the individual indistinctly through the sheet, and he could see that it wasn't a policeman or Jimmy Meideros who entered the room. He appeared to be a very short Spanish man. He was studying Nick's toe tag as if it had fallen out of a UFO or something. He started looking around the room to see which corpse it belonged to. He had his back to Nicholas at the time, so his Columbo routine led to the other side of the room before working back to Nicholas. The man did his rounds and was now standing directly to the left of the not-so-well-disguised, so-called dead guy.

He must have figured out whose toe was not tagged, Nicholas thought to himself while he tried not to laugh. On the guy's shirt it said Laundry Land; a tiny sewn-on tag to the right said Johnny. Nick thought, what a stand-up guy he must be to watch Jimmy's place when he wasn't around to do it himself. Nicholas thought that it would only be appropriate to thank him. As the nervous man reached out to secure the tag to Nick's toe, he appeared to be sweating and shaking. After he'd attached the tag, Nicholas said from under the sheet, "Thank you, my good amigo. Don't my giant feet smell *muy horrible?*" Nicholas then sat up, waving the sheet over his head like a clown in a rodeo, laughing insanely. At that moment, Nicholas discovered that the man was Italian and not Spanish, for Italian obscenities flowed from the man as if he'd just moved here from Italy. He was so scared that he fell down and crawled out of the room, crying. He looked as if he'd been visited by a zombie instead of a giant Swedish kid trying to have some fun. Nicholas got dressed quickly and ran out in the hall to try and calm the frightened man. He felt terrible afterwards and was surprised at himself for doing that to a complete stranger. When Nicholas got out into the long corridor, the Laundry Land man seemed to have vanished into thin air. All that could be heard was the sound of his own stuffed-up nose as he sniffled. Nick then realized that Johnny the laundry guy had a shadow like his. It wasn't as big of course, but he had one.

Nicholas was now faced with the dilemma of finding a way out. The only door he knew of led upstairs to the little man, who was probably going to return with a shotgun or, worse, with the police and a bunch of shotguns. Nicholas looked for a way out. He started toward a room on the other side of the morgue that looked like it was under construction. He stood in the doorway, trying to think of the advice Lynn would give him in a situation like this. First, she would tell him to stay patient, as she always did. Then she would give him an example from her perspective, which was normally pretty sound advice. Nick closed his eyes as he leaned against the doorframe. He missed Lynn very much, more than he cared to admit as a proud strong man. All of a sudden, Nick's daydream was disturbed by a metallic click and a steel barrel pressed to the back of his head. The Laundry Land man had returned armed with a shotgun. Nicholas had premonitions, as everyone does at certain points in life, but rarely of an event happening this rapidly or with such exactitude.

"Get on your stomach with your hands behind your back," the man ordered. His English was perfect when he made this request. Nick attempted to speak. "Shut up. Do you wish you were cremated now?"

He did as he was told, but asked the man a sarcastic question anyway. "I'm curious. Where exactly is Laundry Land, in case I want to take a vacation there someday?" The joke did not spark any laughter, although Nick found it funny when he was thinking it up. His hands and feet were tightly secured with rope. Nicholas looked back at the man from his secured position lying flat on his stomach. "So, Johnny, where's the owner of this joint, Jimmy Meideros?" Johnny had been standing with his foot on Nick's back and the shotgun pointed at his head. He was immediately taken off guard that this strange, undead man knew Jim. Nicholas explained how he knew Jimmy and told a few small tidbits about himself, but not his name. He left out certain parts of the story, of course. Nick didn't mention shadows, alternate worlds, or the fact that he'd woken up in the morgue but hadn't come in through a door or window. He elaborated on their friendship, leaving out the duration of time it had been since he'd actually seen Jimmy. Story time lasted until Nicholas thought it was safe to ask the laundry guy to remove the Tyrannosaurus Rex cannon from the back of his head. Johnny agreed, lowering the rifle. He then told Nicholas to sit against the wall. Nick scooted across the dirty cold floor, once again doing exactly what the man asked him to do.

The man sat across from him about ten feet away. He stared at Nicholas for a short while before asking, "Why were you hiding under the sheet like a dead person?"

"Stress makes people do stupid things. I apologize for scaring you like that." The laundry guy neither declined nor accepted the apology. He simply remained quiet. He was apparently shocked by the whole situation.

Suddenly, the two men heard footsteps rushing down the hall in their direction. It sounded like rubber-soled shoes from the way they squeaked with every quick step. Johnny jumped to his feet, ready for action but keeping his eye on Nicholas. Nick told the guy to calm down, because ghosts and monsters normally don't wear sneakers, so he's probably safe unless it's Dracula. When the man turned the corner, it was Jimmy Meideros himself. From what Nicholas could see Jimmy hadn't changed much over the years. The biggest difference was that he didn't look too happy, so instead of his pearly white smile, he looked stern and concerned. Considering the situation, that was a normal reaction. Nobody likes to be called into a business they own to respond to a tripped alarm or a potential burglar, especially if that place is full of dead people who normally wouldn't be suspects. Jimmy was not accompanied by police or security guards.

Jimmy was now around six feet tall and probably weighed at least two hundred pounds. His hairstyle was much shorter than it had been years before, befitting an older more mature person. He carried a clipboard under his left harm. The suit he wore was steel gray. His tie was black, and though they'd sounded like sneakers, his shoes appeared to be leather. Nicholas imagined that Jimmy was a busy man these days, and he probably had his shoes resoled for comfort, and that explained the squeak.

The first words out of Jimmy's mouth were directed at Johnny. "Please put the shotgun away. Are you injured, Johnny?"

"No," the laundry man replied, "but my ego was a bit wounded by the practical joke that this giant bald man played on me."

"I see. Thanks, Johnny, for treating my property like it was your own. That was very courageous of you. I'll handle it from here, and I'll call you later on to see how you're doing." Johnny proudly accepted the compliment and thanked Jimmy. He then gave Nicholas one last scowl before breaking and unloading his gun and heading off, probably to Laundry Land located somewhere upstairs, Nicholas assumed.

Once Johnny was totally out of sight, Jimmy walked toward Nicholas, who was still sitting on the floor tied up with his back against the wall. "Who the hell are you? And how did you get into my morgue?"

Nicholas was shocked that Jim didn't recognize him. "Jimmy, it's me, from the neighborhood, Nicholas Johansson. Don't you remember me?" Nick was stunned at Jimmy's response, so he couldn't help but laugh at the situation. Jimmy squatted down to examine the intruder's face more closely. All the while, Nicholas kept telling him stories from their past, trying to spark his memory. None of his stories was successful. He didn't hit a sensitive nerve until he mentioned sewer sloshing. Jimmy sat right on the cold dirty floor, expensive suit and all, staring at Nicholas as if he'd seen a ghost. Then his stare suddenly resembled a grin, a grin that Nicholas thought that he had forgotten after all this time. Jimmy quickly untied Nicholas.

As he helped him to his feet, Jim asked, "Nicholas? Where've you been for the last ten years?"

"It's only been about a third of that since my parents' funeral," Nick replied. "Don't you remember, Jimmy?" The smile disappeared from the man's face as he put a few feet between them. Nicholas then brought the conversation back to their last day in the sewer together, just prior to the funeral. "What ever happened to that chick Katrina that you were telling me about that day? Did you guys ever go out on a date?" Jimmy's eyes went wide with fear, and he asked Nicholas once again how he got into the building. The distance between them was now about fifteen feet, as Jimmy realized the difference in their sizes was definitely in Nicholas's favor. Nick could see the situation was going from bad to worse, so he casually sat back down on the floor where he was when he was tied up.

"Look, Jimmy, this may be hard to believe, but I woke up in the morgue, and have no explanation for how I got here." The way things were going, Nick didn't dare bring up anything about murdered homeless men in the sewer. A comment like that might alert the Italian Laundry Land man to return with his shotgun to finish the job.

Jim walked slightly closer and said, "I never went to your parents' funeral or spoke to you about my wife." Jimmy's face looked hot and aggravated.

Nicholas was running out of words to justify his unwelcome appearance. Then Nick was struck with an idea. He began listing people's names from the past, starting with Dr. Reid Anderson and ending with Detective Brian Reilly. All of these people were at the funeral of his parents that Jimmy, for some reason, couldn't remember. Jimmy then wandered past Nicholas and into the room with all the sheets covering the bodies. Nicholas followed, giving the man an adequate amount of breathing room. Jimmy had one hand on his hip with his back to Nicholas as he entered the room. Jim then started flipping page by page through his clipboard, scanning it as he went with his index finger.

He turned to Nicholas. "You're a sick son of a bitch, tampering with the dead."

Nicholas's voice sounded very distressed. "What the hell are you talking about?"

The man threw the clipboard on the floor. "You're a necrophiliac," he said as he began checking under each sheet.

Nicholas was angered by Jimmy accusation, so he demanded, "Talk to me like a man. Don't call me names."

They taunted each other for a while, yelling obscenities back and forth in the way that heterosexual men do when they're releasing anger.

The conversation took a twist when Jimmy kicked over the table that Nicholas awoke on and said, "You're a schizophrenic, a pathological liar."

Nick walked toward him and got up in Jim's face. "What did I ever lie about?"

Jimmy had grown up to be a stand-up person, as Nicholas could see from his response. He looked up, staring hard back into Nicholas's eyes, not backing down for a minute. "You're a liar. Dead people don't attend church on Sunday or grocery shop or see movies or water their grass in the summer. And people don't just wake up in a morgue out of nowhere." He then began checking the rest of the bodies in his morgue.

As Jimmy walked away, Nicholas picked up the table Jimmy had kicked over in his short fit of rage. He sat on it silently, hoping Jimmy would continue where he left off. "Has it really been ten years since you've seen me?" There was no answer. Nick then asked, without bringing up the funeral, "How are my parents? Do they look well?"

Jimmy turned around and faced Nicholas. "You had that accident when you were eight years old, and then you disappeared, like a shadow in the night. When you left, your parents were a wreck, and so were your friends."

Nicholas knew that Jimmy was talking about himself. Nick then jumped off the table. "Why did you choose the word shadow instead of ghost?"

Nick's face looked concerned, so Jimmy felt compelled to answer the insane question. "I don't know. It simply came to mind, that's all. No rhyme or reason."

Nicholas took the answer for what it was and then picked up the clipboard from the floor and handed it to Jimmy. He walked back to the table and sat on it. "Okay, Jimmy, test me on the names from the clipboard."

Jimmy turned around. "Are you truly insane?"

"I'm not a schizophrenic or insane or into necrophilia," he said to his old friend. I simply woke up in the morgue somehow. I'm as confused about the situation as you. All I'm asking for is a test from an old friend to possibly prove a point. That's all."

Jimmy was ready to play the game. "For an old friend, okay. You need to start from the top and list the names. At least I know that you've never seen my clipboard before."

Nicholas had never seen the clipboard before, as Jimmy said. Nor had he pulled any of the sheets off of any of the bodies in the morgue.

He had a funny feeling, an ugly premonition from deep inside. His intuition told him that he knew who was under the sheets, even without looking. Unlike most of his past strange experiences, this time he would have a witness present who could substantiate it as real. His only concern was that by doing this, he might be opening up more problems for himself or for Jimmy.

Nicholas recited the list in alphabetical order, starting with Dr. Reid Anderson and Detective Zack Arbor. Next on the list, both Buggleports, senior then junior. Then Patrick Conley, Oscar Gallo, Theodore Lett, Donna McClennon, and Detective Brian Reilly. Nicholas then asked Jimmy if descriptions or addresses would be necessary in order to get him to listen to what he had to say.

Jimmy looked puzzled as they looked across the room at each other. "Are you a psychic or clairvoyant?" he asked, searching for a logical explanation for what he'd just recited. Jimmy loosened his tie, feeling a bit uncomfortable. Nick then thanked him for giving the test. Though Nicholas didn't want to believe they were true, his horrible answers were actually correct. Nicholas had two more favors to ask his old friend before they parted ways. One favor was to spend another night in the morgue, and the other was for him not to tell his parents that he was alive. Jimmy wanted to deny Nicholas's two requests, attempting to give a moral justification for his decision. Suddenly, before he could finish his explanation, there was a woman's voice calling Jim's name from down the hall. Nicholas thought at first that it was Lynn breaking the boundaries of two worlds to find him. Then he realized that some things are impossible, even for the supernatural.

Jimmy was now in a tight spot of either accepting Nicholas's request or explaining to his wife why he's talking to dead people. Nicholas's face had a deep look of desperation on it, and in the background, Katrina's voice was growing closer. Jimmy said, "Okay. One night for an old friend. But don't destroy any more doors." Nicholas nodded his head as Jimmy snapped the lights off.

As he sat there alone in the dark again, he felt he owed Katrina, a woman he'd never even met, a debt of gratitude for his evening shelter. Nicholas knew now that his parents were alive and well and that the secret was safe with Jimmy. There was no reason to cause them more pain and sorrow than they've already experienced by telling them that their son was alive. Nicholas knew that his future was vastly more undetermined than the average person's. Until he could get that under control, he'd rather remain among the shadows dealing with it alone.

On the other hand, many of his friends, acquaintances, and enemies were dead, and Lynn was lost. Despite his best efforts to make sense of it, the cards fell in a configuration that seemed to have no real pattern. All that's left now was hope, hope that an old friend will appear on a wall and reach out for the hand of another who truly needs to be found.

Shadow Chapter
NUMBER
Fifteen...

Nicholas felt that all of his decisions in life were primarily based on consideration of the well-being of others or their best interest. Many things that took place were out of his control, despite his best efforts. His only true regret was that he was unable to reach more people concerning the shadows. He was unable to visit the prisons or insane asylums to help others understand that what they sometimes see is real, even though reality isn't what it seems to be. Reaching out to others was the basis of Nicholas's motivation to push forward. Spending time with Lynn was at times stressful, emotional, and confusing, like any relationship. Their attachment allowed him to conceive and comprehend the world on the level of both shadows and humans. The experience deepened his human understanding, eliminating fear as a result.

Nicholas was in a room of the dead, the penultimate resting place before preparations for burial began. He lay there in the dark, occasionally looking over at the row of sheets to his left. They were so white that once his eyes adjusted, they seemed to glow in the dark. He took the glow to be a reminder that even in the darkest hour, hope is always there, if you're willing to look for it. Nicholas closed his eyes for a minute, resting his thoughts so as not to over think the situation. Then he sat up, overwhelmed by another idea that totally went against the idea of not over thinking things. He wondered if this was all another test. Waking up paralyzed and freezing in a morgue after being murdered is a test in itself. It's all an attitude test, and Nicholas was absolutely sure that he was on to something big, since he survived it.

In life, every road we choose is adjusted to fit the map of our decision, whether it's good or bad. Even a bad decision can have good consequences if one's attitude is positive. Nicholas felt that all the teachings and influences of the people under the sheets in the room were meant to be. He was there for a reason, at this specific moment in his life and in this specific place. This was not his final resting place. It was merely the final test.

Nicholas lay back down, listening to the caged animal thrashing around in his empty stomach. He hadn't eaten in what seemed like days, even though just the other night he'd eaten like a pig at Florence's hotel in Indiana. The hunger pains became so extreme that they caused him to crunch forward in discomfort. All he could imagine were large pizzas, giant steaks, and one-pound hamburgers.

Nicholas looked around for things to eat. No food was available. He could probably eat his belt if it were real leather. Another option would be to find a mouse and cook it. The only problem was he had no matches or cigarette lighter available. These options would be a last resort if his hunger became unbearable.

The grumbling of Nicholas's stomach quieted, causing his eyelids to relax at the same time. Outside, passing vehicles on the street vibrated the cheap metal tables, creating a steady, relaxing rhythm. Soon the grumbling and vibrating gave way to Nicholas's loud snoring.

Between snores, sometime later, there were four taps on one of the small windows in the room. The taps failed to waken Nicholas, so the Watcher tapped louder and then switched to kicks. A kick from a pointed shoe is a very effective attention getter if done with the proper amount of force and repeatedly. After six consecutive strikes of the shoe against the window, the sleeping giant was awakened by the Watcher outside. Nicholas sat up and screamed like a little girl, invalidating his belief that he had no more fear. His scream was equivalent to the one that Johnny the Laundry Land man released when Nicholas sat up from under the sheet and scared him half to death.

Through the small window, Nick saw what appeared to be a shadow figure lurking behind the tinted glass. Nicholas crouched next to the table after leaping off of it for a second time. The kicking of the window scared the crap out of him, causing him to be startled from his deep sleep. Now that he was awake, all he could dwell on was the bad side of karma. The finger of "what comes around, goes around" was now pointing at him, and it wasn't very funny, not to Nicholas. He realized his practical joke was teaching him an important lesson: "reap what you sow." The swivel handle on the tiny window had a keyhole. Nicholas did not have a key, so he improvised, without causing too much damage this time. He removed the belt that he'd considered eating earlier and used the prong of the buckle to pick the lock, wielding his boot heel as a hammer. One perfectly aligned brutal slam was all that was needed to release the handle. The combination of boot and belt was enough to put the hammer and nails industry out of business, Nicholas thought to himself. He then put his belt back on and opened the window to see who or what was waiting there.

The window was supported by a slow action spring system on either side, causing it to open slowly when the handle was turned. Nicholas was greeted by an old lady on a bicycle. She had a basket attached to the front, with a bell on the handle close to the grip. They stared at each other, each waiting for the other to speak. Nicholas was in a basement, so he was forced to look up in order to see her. Being as tall as he was, this was not something he was accustomed to doing. Finally, the old lady asked Nicholas if the cat had his tongue. Before he could respond, a white cat with beautiful eyes jumped out of the basket and into his arms through the tiny window space. She had a long drawn-out meow and a gentle way about her. Around the kitty cat's neck was a collar with an identification tag attached that read "Molly Gilardi." She purred while Nicholas petted her in the morgue's basement.

"My name is Irene," the woman on the bicycle told Nicholas as he petted the cat. "Have you ever had a pet of your own, Nicholas?"

"How do you know my name? Did Jimmy Meideros or the Laundry Land guy send you over with groceries?"

She seemed not at all insulted by Nicholas not answering her question. "I figured a big guy living in a morgue might be hungry, that's all." She never did answer his question concerning how she knew his name.

Nicholas handed the cat back through the window so she could get back into the basket. Irene then handed Nicholas a brown bag so full of food that it barely fit through the window's opening. Nick thanked the woman, but admitted that he had no money to offer her for it. Nick immediately looked inside the stuffed grocery bag and found an assortment of fruits, granola bars, and tightly wrapped sandwiches. Normally Nicholas would wait until someone was out of view before reviewing the contents of a gift, but in this case his manners became secondary to his overwhelming hunger. At the bottom was a glass bottle of Coke. It was also wrapped in plastic, probably to avoid condensation from seeping through the paper bag. As Nicholas looked inside, Irene said that she owns Irene's Place, a small store and deli located a few blocks away.

Without thinking before he spoke, Nicholas told her that he'd never met an eighty-year-old bicycle delivery lady before. After the words came out, he felt that he should have inserted his foot instead of speaking. He then bit into an apple that was in the bag to avoid blurting out any other poorly thought out ideas. Irene thanked him for the compliment. "In fact," she said, "I'm eight- eight years old, not eighty." Her statement made him feel slightly better.

"And just so you know, in all my years, I've never had to make a delivery to a giant bald Swedish man through a morgue window." The two of them shared a long laugh, as if they'd known each other for years.

Nicholas swallowed his third large bite of apple, its juices dripping down his chin. "How did you know that I was Swedish?" He had forgotten that she also knew his name, something else he'd never told the woman.

Irene smirked. "I've been delivering groceries probably three times as long as you've been alive. In all that time," she explained, "most things really haven't changed that much. The weather may alter slightly, technology may change drastically, but food is food and people are people. And those things never change at all." Nicholas was interested in hearing more from this old lady, who seemed to have infinite knowledge to offer. But right after her last statement, she rang her bicycle bell once and said, "Molly, say bye-bye to our new friend." Molly meowed at Nicholas, then Irene rode away.

Before she was out of earshot, she yelled to Nicholas, "I hope you enjoy the food, but don't eat the wrapper unless you read it first." Nicholas pulled one of the sandwiches out while he held the apple core in his teeth. He proceeded to unwrap it, but there was no message inside, although the Swedish meatballs smelled delicious. The third sandwich was the one that revealed a note attached, which read; "The River NYL runs far and wide. Do you know how to get to the other side?" The words on the note were written in very small handwriting, and Nile was spelt "NYL" for some reason. Nicholas tried to make sense of the note while he filled his face. He stared and stared at it. He studied the acronym NYL, but kept thinking it was NFL. The two were close, after all, and the capital letters were playing mind tricks on tired eyes. He then pictured it in lowercase letters. After that the answer was easy to see. It was a riddle. If the letters were reversed, they spelled "Lyn" with a missing N.

Nicholas returned to the window to see if Irene was possibly hanging around the area making other deliveries. She was unfortunately long gone. Looking through the window, Nicholas noticed the buildings and vehicles in the area. Each of the walls across the street seemed to be alive with shadowy figures. They knew he was in the basement among the dead. But just as they could not enter the cemetery in Indiana, they could not enter the morgue. If they could not come in to visit, maybe they could find a way to draw him out.

Nicholas stuffed Irene's note into his pocket. For the next hour, he wandered the halls of the morgue, mentally making a list of all the signs that were presented to him. Lynn brought the shadow life to Nicholas. Nicholas tried to give shadow life to the world. Shadow life gave Nicholas allies with shadows inside. Shadows led Nick to Indiana. Bad shadows kill Nick. Good shadows bring him back to life in a morgue in Rhode Island. Nicholas was thinking that his facts sounded more like an outline for a self-published book or a scary made-for-television movie. The facts were leading and misleading at the same time. They suggested countless other possibilities, none of which pointed him in a specific direction. His gut instinct told him that Lynn was still obtainable. As long as he hung on to that, the rest of the journey would be worth the trouble.

Nicholas's brief exchange with Irene was much more informative than he could have imagined. After he took the time to read between the lines of what she was saying, it seemed to paint a picture of patience. Patience was a lesson that everyone seemed to preach to him, far more often than he liked to hear it. Irene had been delivering groceries for about fifty-five years, according to what she said, roughly equal to three of his lifetimes, give or take. Irene also said that food is food and people are people, and those things never change at all. Here Nicholas was, boxed in a basement behind tiny windows. He had the weight of the world literally resting on his shoulders. After all, he was standing in a basement under the city. The morgue was oddly a safe place, as Florence Grace's cemetery in Indiana had been. Safety is a feeling of comfort that people take for granted unless there is a cost that helps them estimate its value. Nicholas wished that the cost of his safety wasn't a risk to others. People make exchanges with fate each day of their lives and don't realize the risks they take. Driving down the street in a vehicle full of sparking wires and gasoline is taking a risk. Turning onto an icy road or driving fast on the interstate is another risk. Having improper nutrition is a risk; lack of exercise is a risk. Even the people we associate with as friends, lovers, or acquaintances can pose substantial risks, both physical and mental, if we allow them to. People juggle risks each day, sometimes teetering on the brink of extinction, and they aren't even aware of it. Risks are inevitable, even in our everyday activities of travel, work, and play. How many people have jobs that involve more than everyday risks? Policemen, firemen, and soldiers were a few that came to Nick's mind.

Nicholas started to see all the risks the people in his circle had taken for him. Dr. Reid Anderson basically adopted him. Donna McClennon treated him like he was her own son. Detectives Reilly and Arbor always had his back, no matter what the risk. Lynn gave up her bond with a Compatible to help another. Roslyn altered her own physical appearance for the sake of a shadow friend whom she may have lost forever in her attempt to help him. Patrick Conley gave Nicholas a job and ten thousand dollars. Even if the value of the money meant nothing to the man, the risk of giving it away was worth the good karma he got in return.

What mattered to Nicholas the most was not his own life but the lives of others. His risks revolved around his decisions: would he make the correct decisions now so that others wouldn't have to pay the ultimate cost later. In history, people are often remembered for either selfless deeds or selfish deeds. There are those who commit atrocities and harm mankind, and there are those who give their lives to save it. Nicholas felt honored to be among the latter. He had received a second chance to complete his objective. Florence had guided him back to a safe place, where he could take shelter temporarily and regroup for his final move. When Irene said people don't change, thought Nicholas, she meant that we are creatures of habit. If we continually follow the wrong path, that will be our path, but if we venture out, our path can change.

These thoughts passed through Nicholas's mind as his pacing came to an end. He was now sitting in a dark corner of the morgue, thinking of how he could get out of the building to face the Rippers for the last time. Nicholas stood up and dusted himself off. He then headed back into the room where the bodies lay to say farewell to his friends. His farewell was brief. Nicholas now believed that since angels like Florence and Donna exist, then souls must too. He said a prayer for each of them and thanked them for all they'd done. Nicholas found the door by which Johnny, Jimmy, and Katrina had entered and exited earlier. He never hesitated as he climbed the stairs.

Attempting to leave quietly was not as easy as it sounded. Each stair creaked from the weight of his massive frame. Upstairs, the door was slightly ajar, enough to admit some light around the edges. Nicholas had no idea what was up there. He only knew that from past experience, self-sacrifice was an uncertain risk. The staircase had a total of twelve steps, and Nicholas was now four away from the top. From where he was standing, he was within arm's reach of the door. Nick stopped and closed his eyes, asking for strength from his ancestors to guide him through. When he reopened his eyes, he felt the name Johansson pulsating throughout his veins. The name alone demanded respect, and Nicholas wouldn't accept anything less.

He expected an attack as soon as he opened the door, but there was nothing. All the lights inside the building were out. The light he'd seen around the edges of the door had come from moonlight pouring through a skylight. There were no corpses upstairs, and it seemed devoid of Rippers. The upstairs was also devoid of other humans. All the shades were pulled down; the faint gloom of the streetlights was barely discernible through them. In front of him in the large room that he just entered was a giant picture window, comparable to the one in his living room that he remembered when he was a small boy. Like the others, this window admitted almost no light.

Next to him there was a mirror, just a few feet away from the staircase that he recently climbed. He peered into it in hopes that he would see Lynn through his eyes. As he suspected, she was temporarily gone, but the connection would always be in his heart. As Nicholas turned to go find the exit to the outside, he saw a luminous figure behind the blinds looking in. This time Nicholas walked closer to the shadow. He would not have to go through a side door and attempt a sneak attack as he did when he was eight years old. As he drew closer, he could see that the shadow's dimensions were large. It was as large as the shadow he himself would cast in direct light. Nicholas watched it as it watched him. They stood face to face on either side of the blinds for what seemed like an eternity. Nicholas broke his stare and walked over to the exit. He then unlocked the door to the Meideros Funeral Home, opened it slowly, and stepped out into the night.

The next day's paper had a shocking front-page story that captured the interest of an entire planet. The headline read as follows: "Hundreds in Providence blame accidents on Shadows." The article explained that what we see as the unknown can exist if enough people believe in it together. Strength in numbers is the cornerstone of belief. If the truth is exposed, the unbelievable will no longer be a shameful topic to discuss. The article referred to an accident that took place on July 3, 1988, on the corner of B Street and Thirty-seventh Avenue. A man identified as Nicholas Johansson had been killed within a block of the Meideros Funeral Home. He had been in the process of pulling a family out of a burning car after a three-car pileup occurred in heavy traffic. The cause of this accident, and that of many others that evening, was witnessed by hundreds of people. They all saw shadowy human-like but bodiless figures remove themselves from nearby walls and run into traffic. The sight was horrific and lasted almost twenty minutes, according to the testimonies of countless frightened witnesses. Many people were attacked as others watched in fear, not comprehending how to react. Within hours, similar events were reported throughout the world, as far away as Australia. This tragic event in tiny Rhode Island became a reason for people the world over to stand up and face their fears by exposing their secrets to the world. Our universe can change in an instant, altering life as we know it forever. Fortunately, many had the opportunity to witness the event in Rhode Island.

After the commotion died down, there was a single vehicle left lying sideways in the road as a result of the accident in Providence. Its headlights were shining on a wall, creating a stage of sorts in front of the gathering crowd.

There they saw a man and woman, standing together in the shadows, holding hands. Neither of their shadowy figures was cast by a human body. They did not attempt to run or hide or conceal themselves in any way. They stood silently and perfectly still. They stood on the wall long enough for all who were watching to comprehend that what they were seeing was real.

Nicholas Johansson's selfless sacrifice allowed him to be granted a new beginning. From this day on and for all eternity, he would remain in perfect harmony alongside the shadow of a murdered girl named Monica Lamestra, whom he called Lynn, originally out of desire and now in eternal love. She was meant to be his lady for endless time or until time ceased to exist. Nick and Lynn set an example for all mankind to see, first with their hearts and then with their minds.

He'd risked everything to prove to the mortal world that shadows do exist. His efforts gave hope to a shadow group called Faith Finders, letting them know that many of us can see them and that we are thankful for their concern.

The End